I Didn't Get to Say Goodbye

Copyright © 2024
All Rights Reserved
A High Pines Press Publication

Printed in the United States of America

In accordance with the U.S. Copyright Act of 1976, the scanning, uploading, and electronic sharing of any part of this book without the permission of the publisher/author constitute unlawful piracy and theft of the author's intellectual property.

This book is a work of fiction. Names, characters, places, and incidents are either the product of the author's imagination or are used fictitiously, and any resemblance to actual persons, living or dead, business establishments, events, or locales is entirely coincidental.

Format and Cover Design deboraklewis@yahoo.com
Cover photo courtesy Shutterstock.com

ISBN: 9798342038089

I Didn't Get to Say Goodbye

B.B. MONTGOMERY

Acknowledgements

I am a fact-to-fiction writer and when my dear friend Diana came to me with a file full of newspaper articles about the murder of two wives, I couldn't resist. Of course, I changed the names to protect the innocent and took a writer's creative license to create a murder mystery with several unexpected twists. I can't forget Sandy, the inspiration for the main character Laura. How fun it was to create her persona.

I never take credit for doing this alone. I have leaned on my editor Tenita for the last seven books and am excited for the efforts of my new editor Gretchen. She has been strict with her comments but nothing I can't handle. I love her professionalism and expertise.

This is the first book in the Cold Case Series and I await your reviews and opinions. I am already creating the next book in the series. Look for it soon.

Bob is and has been the most important source for my writing. His input is most valuable. I love him.

Prologue

"Laura, I've got to see you!"

The urgency in her sister's voice stopped her in her tracks. "Vicky, what's wrong?"

"I can't tell you over the phone. I'll meet you down at Charley's. Please, say you'll come!"

"I'm right in the middle of painting my bathroom. Can you wait about an hour?"

Hearing her sister's whine on the other end of the line, Laura quickly put the lid back on the paint can. "Never mind, I'll be right there."

Trying to ignore the bad feeling in her gut, Laura pulled the red bandana off her head and attempted to restore some decency to her hair. She finally gave up and put it up in a big clip. As she headed out the door, she noticed a light rain was coming down. She pulled her truck slowly onto the slick roads but, ignoring her own thoughts about driving safely and recalling her sister's panic, Laura quickly headed to the little bar just up the road. Charley's Tavern & Grill was a local hangout with a great pizza menu and drinks in a no-frills atmosphere. The sisters had met there over the years as it was halfway between their respective homes in Prescott, Arizona. It was their special place to talk and catch up on each other's lives. This might not be one of those pleasant talks, she thought morosely.

The early spring weather very often gave way to showers in this high mountain community of about 50,000 people. Laura had moved to this beautiful town after her divorce from Carl six years ago. He stayed in the valley in their big home in Carefree while she longed for a smaller place to call her own.

Finding a parking spot close to the front door, Laura noticed that Vicky's car was already parked on the side of the building. Grabbing her purse, she hurried into the darkened interior of the bar. She saw her sister right away and headed over to greet her. "Hey, you made it fast."

"I called you from here." Vicky tipped up her drink. "I ordered some wine for you." She pushed a stemmed glass over. "Love the hairdo. When are you going to give up that bright red dye?"

"It looks like you've been here a while." Laura indicated several empty glasses on the table, ignoring the remarks about her hair. "What's going on?"

Before answering, her sister swallowed the last few sips. "I need you to promise me something."

"That sounds ominous. What has you so upset?" Laura took a sip of the white wine, anxiously waiting for Vicky to speak and give her more of an explanation.

"I know that you've never been a fan of Randy." Vicky spoke in whispered tones about her husband.

"That's not exactly true. I just don't like how he treats you sometimes." She reached over and patted her sister's hand.

The tears were falling freely now from Vicky's eyes, and she used the bar napkin to wipe at them, ignoring the mess she was making with her makeup. Taking another sip of her drink, she continued, "Well, you may have been right all along."

"What in the world has happened?" She asked.

"We've been fighting for quite some time now. I won't tell you any of the gruesome details, but I'm planning to leave him soon." She was sobbing and had to take a few moments to compose herself.

"You two have been together for almost ten years. Can't you work it out?"

"Oh, Laura, you're such an optimist. Once it's broken, it can't be fixed." She signaled the bartender to bring more drinks over.

"Are you sure you should drink more?"

"I can't be drunk enough with what I have to tell you."

"Now you're scaring me. I can't imagine what has you so upset."

"Here's the thing. If you ever hear of me disappearing into thin air, don't you for one minute believe it!" Vicky pointed her finger at her.

There was a silence between them for a bit. Each of the women appeared deep in their own thoughts. Finally, after they got the drinks, Laura tried once again to reason with her sister. "Vicky, please tell me why you said that. I'm scared for you."

"I want you to promise me that you'll not let him get away with anything."

"I promise, but you're going to have to give me more information."

"You know that Randy was married before?"

"Yes, you told me that. What's that got to do with what's happening now?"

"I think he killed her."

One

After trying desperately to convince her sister to come home with her, Laura finally gave up and left by herself. She secured a promise from Vicky to call her, no matter what time, day or night, if she needed to talk. It was difficult to get back into her project, but hard work had always been a cure to keep her mind busy. She stirred the paint and started the tedious task of cutting in the new color on the walls of her guest bathroom.

After several mistakes, she finally gave up and went to work on the computer. Her subconscious mind took over and soon she found one small article about Randy's first wife. Everything she saw indicated that Donna just disappeared and was never found. The story located on a back page of the newspaper simply stated that Randy cooperated with the investigation and was not a suspect. It was determined to be a closed case with no solution. When her cell chimed, Laura saw that it was Vicky.

In a whispered voice her sister spoke, "Hey, Sis, just ignore me. Don't take anything I said seriously. I'm not a happy woman right now but I'll fix it."

"It's hard to ignore. You made some pretty serious allegations. I don't want you to stay in a dangerous situation. Come and live with me until you figure things out." She made one more attempt.

"I'll be fine. Don't worry. I just needed someone to listen to my pathetic ramblings. I'll call you in a day or two."

The call ended, but her nagging thoughts didn't. She searched further but finally admitting a dead end, Laura went to bed.

The next morning found her at the sheriff's office. Taking a deep breath for moral support, Laura went through the doors and up to the window.

"Can I help you?" A young, uniformed man asked from behind the glass partition.

"I'm investigating a woman's disappearance from about fifteen or twenty years ago. Do you have anyone who I could talk to about that?"

"Do you have her name?" He appeared patient with her request.

"Donna Bell. I don't know much more than that." She smiled.

He typed on the keyboard in front of him and when something came up on the screen, the polite young man looked up. "This case was moved to cold cases. The detective has since retired and I'm afraid that's all I have for you."

"Can I have the detective's name?" She smiled again.

"I'm sorry, but we can't give out that information."

"I really just want to talk with him. How about you give him my name and number? Perhaps he can call me."

The young deputy passed a small piece of paper through the bottom of the window. "Write your name and number on here. I'll pass the information on and if he wants to talk with you, he'll call."

Without much hope for a call back, Laura left her number and a small note about what she was looking for from the detective. As she left the building, Laura noticed the sky was clearing. Feeling the need for some exercise, she decided to walk to the Jersey Lilly Saloon where she worked part-time on an as-needed basis. Laura knew they didn't open until later, but she could check on her upcoming schedule.

Just as she was taking the stairs, her cell chimed, and Laura stopped to answer. "Laura Shepherd?" The male voice on the other end asked.

"Yes. Who is this?"

"I'm Patrick Dickson."

"I don't think I know you." She was hesitant. "I don't normally answer calls from unknown numbers." She was about to end the call when he quickly added, "I was one of the investigators on the Donna Bell missing case."

"Wow! I wasn't sure I would hear from you, let alone this fast." She stopped and waited.

"Can we meet?"

"I'm available now if you'd like."

"I can meet you. Where?" His voice was deep and sure, full of confidence.

"How about downtown at the courthouse? I will be sitting on the base of the Bucky O'Neill statue." She was amazed that this man wanted to meet so quickly but it also alerted her senses to some impending danger.

Turning about, she headed back down the stairs and walked quickly across the street to the courthouse. This area wasn't as crowded on weekdays, and she found herself at the renowned statue. Bucky O'Neill died in his service with Teddy Roosevelt as one of the famous Rough Riders from San Juan Hill. It was visited by many tourists as a sight to see in Prescott.

She sat down and tried to appear calm as she awaited the detective. He wasn't hard to recognize as she watched a tall, dark-headed man wearing the usual western cowboy hat coming towards her. Instantly, Laura wished she'd taken the time to comb her unruly red locks and perhaps change her blouse to something less casual.

Sitting up straighter, she tried to appear confident and less intimidated. He wore dark sunglasses which hid his eyes. Laura considered the eyes as the window to a person's soul and was a bit dismayed that she couldn't see his.

"Laura Shepherd?" He reached out his hand to shake hers.

"Detective Dickson?" She stood and met his grip. "I have to be honest. I didn't expect such a fast response. That young deputy must have called you right away about my note."

"Let's go over here and we can sit." The detective pointed to a bench close by. "I'm not active in the sheriff's office anymore. I retired from there about ten years ago." He took off the sunglasses and she finally had a glimpse into the soul of Patrick Dickson. Laura liked what she saw.

"Why are you here then?"

"One of the things I hate is when I have unfinished business, especially in the sheriff's office. This was one of the few cases I never solved."

"And it bothers you to this day." She stated firmly.

The fact that he didn't respond confirmed what she felt she knew.

"Why are you looking into this case?" he asked bluntly.

"I'd rather not say right now, but I need to find out more about her disappearance. I guess you could say it's for personal reasons."

"Did you know her?"

"No." She knew he wanted more, but to protect her sister, Laura was not sure she should trust the big man sitting next to her. "Can you share any information with me?"

"I can tell you that the case was basically closed a long time ago."

"I know that much from the internet. They never found any trace of her. Weren't there any suspects? Was there any evidence of foul play?"

He now turned and looked directly at her. "You sound as though you might have some information the authorities didn't at the time."

Now it was her turn to be uncomfortable. How much do I give him? Her thoughts whirled around in her head. "I don't really."

"What prompted you to look into this? Why after sixteen years are you interested?"

"Can't you just trust me for now? Please, I don't have any added information. I'm simply curious."

"Have you eaten? I'm hungry." He stood.

His abrupt change of topic confused her. She stammered out a reply. "I guess I could eat. Where?"

"The Lone Spur has a great lunch menu." He pointed to a building across the street from the courthouse plaza.

"I've eaten there. It is good."

Together they walked side by side and as they entered the restaurant, the hostess greeted him with a huge smile and immediately took them to a table in the back.

The server greeted Patrick, "Hey, I haven't seen you in a long time."

"It's been a while. How's your son doing?"

She smiled and filled him in on the antics of her teenager. "I can't thank you enough, Patrick. You saved us from disaster."

With a wave of his hand, he dismissed her praise. "I'm glad to hear that things are going well."

With that the server turned to Laura to see what she wanted to eat. Laura ordered a burger and fries and waited for him.

Once the server left them on their own, Patrick finally spoke. "I was suspicious about the disappearance of his wife but could never prove anything. There was no evidence, no body and no crime scene. It sticks in my craw to this day."

A feeling of impending doom invaded her being. Laura felt that her sister was definitely in danger even though her call late last night was to convince her otherwise. "My sister is married to Randy Bell."

She waited for a reaction from him, but Patrick held his composure for a bit. In his own good time, he turned to face her. She saw some hesitation, but finally he spoke. "You obviously have some concerns. Why?"

In for a penny, in for a pound, thinking about words her grandmother would speak. Taking a sip of her coffee before answering, Laura looked at the tall, good-looking man seated across from her. His concern for the server and her son showed Laura that this was a man who could be trusted. "She told me something just yesterday that chilled me to the bone."

The food appeared at that moment, delaying the rest of their conversation. She took a bite of the burger and found that she was hungrier than originally thought. Patrick was crumbling crackers into his chicken noodle soup. They were both caught up in their own thoughts and food.

Finally setting her burger down and wiping her hands and mouth with the napkin, Laura answered his question. "I want you to understand that my sister and I are close, and her disclosure has me very worried."

"I can appreciate that."

"While I haven't always approved of his behavior, Randy has never given me the idea that he would harm her in any way."

"Until?" Patrick prompted.

"Until last night. She called me to meet her and when I got there, she had already been drinking. She told me that they had not been getting along and she was thinking of leaving her husband."

He nodded but didn't interrupt her thoughts with his questions.

"I did my usual big sister thing and tried to talk her into getting them to work things out. When I saw that it was more serious, I offered her to stay at my place." Pushing her food aside, Laura found her appetite was suddenly gone.

"You're a good sister."

That comment was almost her undoing. Laura turned her head to hide the tears forming in her eyes. She looked back at him. "I try to be. I'm sorry if my emotions are showing, but my sister is one of the most important people in my life."

"Never apologize for loving family."

"She told me that she thinks Randy killed his first wife." There, she dropped the bomb.

"Are you ready to get out of here?" Patrick waited just a second for her answer. When she nodded, they got up. He left a stack of bills on the table and with his hand lightly at her back, they left and went out the front door.

"What now?" She asked him.

"Do you have some time? There's something I'd like to show you." Patrick proposed.

Just as she was about to answer, Laura heard, "Nana! What in the world are you doing here?"

"Sunny, I think the better question is, what are you doing here? Shouldn't you be in school?" Laura turned just in time to see the surprised look on Patrick's face as the perky teenager came up and hugged her grandmother.

"Who's this good-looking guy?" Sunny asked with a big smile on her face.

"Sunny, mind your manners." Laura tried to control her vivacious granddaughter.

Patrick offered his hand. "I'm Patrick."

"Are you a friend of my Nana's?" The youngster pushed for information as she shook his hand.

"I think we could become good friends. We actually just met today." He grinned as he enjoyed her energy.

"Well, I'm Sunshine. My grandmother calls me Sunny." She turned back to Laura, "And to answer your question, I'm not in class today. I came downtown to find a part-time job. One of my friends told me they were hiring here in the Lone Spur."

"Well, you better get on in there. I'll talk with you later, Sweetie." Laura gave her a small peck on the cheek and laughed when Sunny winked at her.

"Oh, yeah, we'll talk for sure. It was really nice to meet you, Patrick." Sunny bounded off into the restaurant.

Feeling the awkward moment, Laura laughed nervously. "She's a lively one."

"You don't look old enough to have a granddaughter that age." His compliment made her blush.

"Do you have any grandchildren?" She tried to make light conversation. As they stood there on the sidewalk, several people walked by, window shopping at the various local shops. This area across from the courthouse plaza was a regular tourist stop for the many visitors enjoying the spring Prescott weather.

"No, we had two children, but they don't seem to want to oblige me with grandchildren."

"I love Sunny. She's my only and we are very close. She moved up here to go to college. It keeps her near to me, so I can keep an eye on her. Most women love being a grandmother. I bet your wife would love it, too."

"Amy died ten years ago." He stated without emotion.

"Oh, I'm sorry. I didn't mean..." Laura stammered her apology.

"No worries. She had been ill a long time and it was rather a blessing. I've gotten used to not having her around." He walked to a nearby bench and sat down. "I don't mean to sound harsh, but she'd been in such pain for so long. It was terribly frustrating to just stand by and not be able to help her."

"I can only imagine." Trying to get back to a more comfortable and less personal topic, Laura reminded him. "You said there was something you wanted to show me."

"If you have the time. I'm free right now."

"Sure, where are we going?"

"I have some information in my home office that I think you would be interested in about that unsolved case."

"That would be great. I just want to help my sister and if she needs to get away from her husband, more knowledge may help her make the hard decision to leave."

He stood. "Do you want to follow me? I live close by, just across from the Dells. I'll text you my address and you can use your GPS to find it in case you lose me. I've been told I drive too fast." The grin on his handsome face did funny things to her insides which she chose to ignore.

"I'll follow you." She looked at her phone as it chimed and saw his address pop up on the screen. "See you there."

She felt a little less anxious as she walked to her truck alone, away from Patrick. She hadn't expected the detective to be handsome and single.

Not that it mattered, she thought to herself. Laura had no intentions of ever getting involved again. She'd been married at fifteen and once divorced from Carl, swore she would be quite content to be on her own. Thinking of Carl made her smile. The years with him had been okay, but the love waned a long time before the divorce and they both knew it. They were still friendly as they shared time with their son, Josh and granddaughter. Carl's generosity with the divorce settlement allowed her financial independence, for which she was very grateful.

Getting out of the downtown square could be a challenge as traffic was always busy there, but she managed to get moving and saw Patrick get into his truck just ahead. He drove up to Highway 89 and with a little effort, Laura followed him right to his home.

The Granite Dells was a section just about four miles out of downtown and close to two local lakes, Watson Lake and Willow Creek Lake. It was a fairly new development and as she drove, Laura marveled at the large, custom-built homes on each side of the road. Patrick turned left and she found herself fascinated with homes that appeared to be built directly on the rocks with the beauty of nature surrounding each structure.

Pulling her car right behind his, she got out and admired the view. "This is a beautiful location. How did you find this?"

The garage door opened as he answered, "I found this lot years ago and when I retired, I started to build the house. It's taken me a couple of years to finally get it done."

"Oh, wow! I bet that was fun." She walked into the garage and suddenly noticed a huge boulder jutting from the wall on the left. "Look at that! You put the wall right around the rock. Why didn't you just remove it?"

He spoke proudly. "I wanted to blend in with the natural environment rather than fight it. Wait until you see the rest of the house." He opened the door and waited for Laura to enter. As they moved down the hallway to the kitchen area, she marveled at the attention to detail he'd put into his home.

"What's the square footage for the house?" She ran her hand over the smooth granite countertops, admiring the neutral colors with splashes of blues and yellows in the paintings and accents around the room. The many windows allowed the sunshine to lighten up the entire area.

"The total is about 5,000 square feet with five bedrooms and three bathrooms. There is a complete game room and a theatre set up downstairs. Check out this deck and view." He pulled open the sliding glass door and together they stepped out onto a huge deck that encompassed the entire back and sides of the house.

"Detective, this is amazing. From this view, you wouldn't know there were any other houses in the area." She stared out at the mountains in the distance and admired the rocks and trees surrounding them. There was a slight hint of car noises coming from the highway below, but it was very subtle. "What is this deck made of?" She bent down and ran her hand across the smooth planks.

"Please call me Patrick. It's a composite made of 95% recycled materials. It's an alternative to the traditional redwood used on most decks. The beauty of it is that it never has to be sealed or treated. You put it down and forget it." His voice carried a certain amount of pride.

"I have a small deck on the back of my place, but you wouldn't dare walk on it with bare feet. This would be a wonderful fix for it."

"Where is your house?"

"I'm a couple of blocks east of Mt. Vernon Street, on South Pleasant Street. I bought an old fixer-upper and have been diligently working to restore it over the last six years." She laughed and added, "It's been a huge learning process for me."

"You sound as though you're enjoying it." He leaned against the railing and watched the look of joy spread over her face as she talked.

"Oh, I am in heaven. I've figured out that you just don't have limitations if you put your mind to it. That's something I've been trying to teach Sunny. She's so eager to learn everything she can about life."

"It was a pleasure to meet her. She looks like you."

Laura reached up and fluffed her unruly hair. "She can have this too if she wants. It comes in a bottle." Her laughter was spontaneous, and he joined in with her amusement.

"I think it suits you."

His compliment was another unexpected one and she found herself on unfamiliar ground. The only man in her life from the time she was fifteen was Carl and he was a man of few words, let alone words that were said to please a woman.

"Do you want to show me that information? I have a bathroom waiting for paint back home." She nervously tried to joke away her discomfort.

"Yeah, let's go back down the hallway. My office is there. I do want to warn you, though. Most people decorate their offices or dens with trophies or certificates of accomplishment, but mine is more a work in progress. Come, I'll let you be the judge."

She was close behind but took in the various rooms on the way back towards the garage. When he came to a closed door, she saw him hesitate before opening it. Once he did, he stood back and motioned for her to step into what seemed to be his sanctuary.

She could feel him watching her reaction as Laura stepped further into the room. She looked around and took in the fact that all four walls were covered with pictures, newspaper articles, documents, maps, and other types of information listed on whiteboards and bulletin boards. "Is this all about the Donna Bell case?"

"No, each wall represents the four cases I could never solve. Every one of these walls holds all the evidence I gathered. I don't want you to think that I'm some kind of nutcase that can't let go. It's not an ego thing, either. I got to know the people involved and affected by these crimes and there's a part of me that won't rest until I can help successfully close each one of these. When I heard you went into the sheriff's office, I got very excited that perhaps I could get one of the walls cleared off."

She wandered over and found the wall that represented Donna Bell's case. "Oh, my God. I've been in that house." She pointed to a picture on the wall.

"That's where Donna and Randy lived when she disappeared. How do you know that place?"

Laura sat on the only chair in the room. "When my sister married Randy, she moved into his home and they lived there for about four years. I never realized that he had been there with his first wife." With more thought, she added, "I wonder if Vicky realizes that?"

"Randy and Donna bought that place at a really low price and after four years with your sister, he sold it and tripled his investment. Your sister and

Randy then moved up to their big home off Lee Boulevard." He stated facts and watched for her reaction. I know they both make good money, but the facts and figures don't add up to supporting them in that lifestyle." He dropped that tidbit of information on her.

"What are you suggesting?" She challenged him.

"I'm not suggesting anything, just presenting the questions that remain unanswered. What are you thinking?" He put it right back to her.

She stood up, having regained her composure. "I would want to know who you talked with back when his wife disappeared. I want to know what sort of searches were done. I think you need to fill me in on all the details that you have so far."

With a smug sort of smile on his face, Patrick proceeded to explain each of the documents on the wall. Laura saw a picture of Donna Bell and stopped. "She looks very similar to my sister. That's weird."

"I have a theory about that if you're interested."

"You're testing me, aren't you? You want to see how much I really want to help my sister." She stood up. "I think I need to go. This is all going to take a bit of processing."

"I understand. You have my number. Give me a call when you want to talk again." They both walked back to the garage where she headed for her truck.

Laura turned to speak. "I thank you for meeting me. I really do have a lot of thinking to do about all of this. I want to talk with my sister again."

"I understand." He repeated.

As she backed up, Laura tried to not think about the man she had just met and the fact that he might be the help she needed to get her sister out of a volatile situation.

The route back to her place didn't take long and as she pulled into her driveway, Laura noticed her granddaughter's car parked on the curb. She went in the side door and saw Sunny sitting at the breakfast bar.

"Nana! I wasn't sure you'd be home so soon." The twinkle in her eyes indicated her curiosity.

"Young lady, you're incorrigible!"

"Nana, who was that good-looking man? How did you meet him?" She took a sip of her soda. With a giggle, she asked, "Is he going to be my new grandpa?"

Laura stopped in the middle of helping herself to a glass of iced tea. "You are in so much trouble, young lady!"

"Seriously, Nana, you should have a boyfriend. I hate to think of you all alone."

Before answering her, Laura took a long sip of her drink. "I'm perfectly happy being alone. I was with your grandfather Carl forever and now I am here, on my own and very, very happy!"

"Methinks you doth protest too much!" Sunny laughed out loud.

"Oh, that's what we get for sending you to college. You've learned to misquote Shakespeare."

"Seriously, Nana, he seemed really nice. How did you meet him?"

Laura didn't want to lie to her but felt that Sunny didn't need to know everything. "I was researching something, and he was recommended to me as a good resource."

"Does this have anything to do with Aunt Vicky and her husband?"

Two

"What do you mean?" Laura pretended innocence.

"Oh, Nana, you're so cute when you try to act like I shouldn't know family secrets." Sunny laughed at the sour expression on her grandmother's face.

"What are we going to do with you?" She hugged Sunny to her side. "I love you, but seriously, child, you've got to learn when to keep your mouth shut. Some things in the family are not for your tender ears to hear."

Changing the subject, Laura asked, "Did you get the job?"

"I did! Isn't that great? I already met one of the other servers and she told me that Patrick is a retired cop. That's why I figured it had to do with Uncle Randy and his dark past."

"You're not going to let this go, are you?" Laura reached for the pitcher and refilled her glass. "Tell me what you know."

"I know that Uncle Randy was married before and that his first wife just disappeared. I know that Aunt Vicky isn't very happy right now."

"How do you know that she's unhappy?"

"She calls my dad and talks with him. I hear his end of the conversation, but he doesn't tell me anything. He doesn't trust me like you do. You know that I can keep my mouth shut. We've shared secrets and to this day, I've never told anyone about any of them." She spoke proudly of herself.

"Thanks for that. It is nice to have some special secrets between us, isn't it?" Laura smiled.

"That's why you can tell me about Patrick and why you wanted to talk with a cop about Uncle Randy."

"Oh, Sunny, I will let you know more when I find out some facts. Right now, I just met with him to find out what he knows. He was the original detective on the case when Randy's first wife disappeared." When she saw the intent look on her granddaughter's face, she added, "Now, don't go getting ideas. People disappear off the face of the earth all the time and sometimes it's because they want to. It doesn't necessarily mean something suspicious happened."

"I believe you. Promise me that you'll let me know what you find out. I gotta go now. My dad expects me to fix dinner and I still have to go to the store." She jumped up and kissed Laura on the cheek. "Love you, Nana. Remember! I want to know what you find out." Her voice was fading with her words as she dashed out the side door.

"I remember when I had that kind of energy." She spoke to an empty room. Deciding that she needed to finish the bathroom, Laura changed into her painting clothes and was working away when her phone chimed. Wiping her hands free from paint, she saw that it was her sister.

"Hey, Vicky. How are things today?" She tried an upbeat tactic.

"I just wanted to say again that I am sorry for venting to you yesterday."

"Hey, it's what sisters are for, right? Things alright?" Laura wasn't convinced.

"About the same. I just wanted to make sure you wouldn't worry. I know how my big sister can be when she hears of trouble or something that needs fixing. Randy and I will work this out, I'm sure." Vicky tried once again to take back the words she spoke yesterday.

Deciding to take the higher road, Laura spoke encouraging words, "I know you two will figure things out. Please, just call me if you need someone to talk to or join you for another drink." She tried to make a joke.

Once the call was finished, Laura stood back and looked at the fresh paint on her walls. When she bought the house, every wall seemed to have a different color. The first room she repainted was her bedroom. The walls were now a soothing creamy white, not purple. This bathroom, even as small as it was, had bright yellow on each wall but one. The wall over the tub had been painted a bold, almost fluorescent orange.

She had to use a primer and then apply two coats of a soft beige. Laura admired her work and was happy with the results. She still needed to paint the wall over the tub, but feeling her back muscles screaming at her, Laura sealed up the paint and put her brush and roller in plastic bags for tomorrow.

As the sun was setting, Laura took a bottle of water from the fridge and opened the sliding glass door to her deck. She looked down at the warped, splintered boards and suddenly remembered the deck surrounding Patrick's house. That might be my next project, she reflected. Sitting down on a lounge chair, Laura sipped the chilled water and admired the red and purple hues as the sun slowly made its descent onto the horizon.

She felt at peace here in her own backyard. All the hard work she'd already done and the many more tasks ahead were the very thing she'd craved for years. With the divorce, her dreams could be realized. Crickets were chirping their evening songs and a few barks from neighboring dogs could be heard, but for the most part, it was heaven to Laura.

As she sat there, her mind wandered back to the whiteboard on the wall in Patrick's home office. She tried to recall the information she had seen but failed. Laura made a decision at that moment. She got up, and walking into her own little office, grabbed a marker. The walls in this room had not yet been painted, so she started her own lists, scribbling her thoughts directly on the light blue paint.

She created a list and labelled it 'questions' that needed answers. She started another list and called it 'witnesses' who needed to be interviewed again. The third list was one that included places that needed to be revisited, and she named it 'crime scenes'. As she stood back and studied her work,

Laura noted that it wasn't professional, but it made complete sense to her.

Checking the time on her phone, Laura hit the button and called Patrick.

His rich voice answered promptly, "Laura. I didn't expect to hear from you so soon."

"I hope it's not too late. I, myself, am a night person."

"No, this is fine. What's on your mind?" Patrick prodded.

"I've made my own lists and wondered if you'd like to see them?" She wasn't sure how he'd react.

"Somehow, I thought you might. Do you want to meet and compare notes?" He suggested.

"Well, I can't exactly bring them to you. I could take a picture with my phone, but I'd rather you see them for yourself. Are you busy tomorrow morning, say around ten?"

"I can free up some time."

"There's something else I'd like to get your advice about if you don't mind." She thought of the deteriorating wood on her deck.

"Sure. Should I bring some bear claws?"

She almost giggled like a schoolgirl. How could he possibly know that bear claws were her favorite pastry? "That would be fine. I'll text my address to you. See you then."

Deciding what to fix for dinner reminded Laura that her granddaughter was supposed to fix that meal for her dad. She punched her son's number. "Josh, how are you doing, son?"

"Mom, I was just finishing my dinner."

"Oh, then, Sunny came through." She laughed.

"If you call dinner a takeout meal from that new chicken place by the mall, then I guess she came through."

"She's something else, isn't she?" Laura prompted.

"Mom, she's the best daughter a man could ask for, but sometimes I could just strangle her. She's so smart at school, but handling everyday tasks, argh!" His frustrations were evident.

Laura's laughter stopped his rant. "Josh, when you were a little boy, I said a silent prayer that when you became a father, you would have a child just like you. I didn't mean it, but it certainly came true, didn't it?"

He quickly joined in her fun. "I was that much to handle?"

"Yes, and more. Josh, just enjoy her now. Soon she'll find her own way and we'll be left behind."

"Mom, she'll always be your little Sunny and you know it. What's going on?"

"Nothing, really. I've been working on the house and perhaps I'm a little tired. That's all."

"I don't believe it, not for one minute. You love working on that little palace of yours." Josh answered.

"Well, there is one thing. Have you spoken with Vicky lately?" She hoped her question sounded innocent enough.

"Yeah, we talked just the other day. Why do you ask?"

"We met at Charley's and she seems rather unhappy. Did she say anything to you?"

He answered right away. "Mom, you know Randy aggravates the hell out of her. He's gone a lot and she's left on her own. Her mind gets too active and then they fight."

"Why's he gone so much? I wasn't aware of that." Laura asked her son.

"Vicky thinks he's seeing someone. I told her that was absurd, but he only knows he's off somewhere and she hasn't a clue what he's doing. They don't communicate very well."

"That's the way it is in most relationships, isn't it? Your father and I never seemed to talk except for trivial day-to-day things. When I tried to talk about my feelings, he just clammed up. Oh, well, son, I better go and find something for my own dinner. Talk to you later. Love you!" They ended the call.

After finding some quick snacks of cheese and crackers, Laura found herself ready for bed. Snuggling down in her covers, with the television on her favorite channel, Laura settled down for the night.

One of the things she loved most about her home was the fact that the rising sun helped get her up in the morning each day. She indulged in automatic shades that worked with the remote by her bed. If she wanted to sleep in a bit longer, she could just lower them without much effort. This morning, however, she wanted to be up and ready to show her work to Patrick.

"Alexa, play some classic country." She gave instructions to the technology sitting next to her television. Laura grinned as she thought about the day Sunny gave her the device. They had a fun time setting it up with Sunny showing her how it worked. She was surprised how much she'd gotten used to having Alexa in her home.

Once she checked the time, Laura put on some coffee and opened the sliding door to the back deck. The air was fresh with a slight breeze. Taking a deep breath, she once again thanked the good Lord for being able to live in this town and have her own little home.

Promptly at ten, she heard a knock on the front door and found Patrick there with a box of goodies in his hand. "Right on time. I expected nothing less."

He tipped his hat as he entered the living room. "I always aim to please." Patrick handed her the box as they went to the kitchen and he put his hat on the breakfast bar stool. Trying not to notice how handsome he was without that hat blocking his eyes, she reached for a mug. "How do you take your coffee?"

"Just black. I try to keep things simple."

Grabbing some napkins and handing him the hot coffee, she opened the screen door, and they went to sit out on the deck. "This is a nice backyard. Those hedges all around give you quite a bit of privacy. I like that."

"It's one of the things that convinced me that this was the house for me. The house my ex and I lived in down in Carefree was huge with an acre lot and sweeping views. I somehow couldn't see myself in a regular neighborhood and this place does the trick."

"You have an ex-husband?" His question seemed casual enough.

"Yes, we've been divorced a little over six years now. Joshua was our only child and he's the father of my little Sunshine." She took a bite of the delicious-looking pastry. "This is good. Where did you get them?"

"There's a little bakery just off the courthouse square. It's kind of hard to find, but they bake the best cakes, cookies, and pastries. They sell out fast, so you have to get there early. Remember, cops always know where to find the best donuts," he joked.

His rich wholesome laughter was catching, and Laura found herself enjoying his sense of humor.

"This is the deck I was telling you about. See how bad the wood is?" She changed the subject.

"At one time, this was probably beautiful. If you don't seal it every year, this is what you get. That's a shame." He put his hand down to rub across the rough wood.

"Could I put down that composite material you have on your deck?" She put the question to him.

Patrick got up and walked all around, checking the entire space. "You'll want to rip all the old decking off and then check for the structural integrity of the frame. If everything's in good shape, then it's just a matter of putting the new boards down. You need to make sure the distance between the joists is sixteen inches. Normally redwood requires two feet, so you might have to add some extra boards to meet the requirements for composite. It's going to be a lot of work." He looked at Laura, sizing up her work ethic. "Although, I think you're a woman who is not afraid of hard work."

"You got that right. Could you help me measure so I know how many boards to buy?"

"Sure, you have a tape measure?" He corrected himself, "Of course you have a tape measure."

She went inside and came right back out with a pad and pen and the requested equipment. They spent the next several minutes measuring the area. She wrote down the figures as he measured them and when they were finished, he took the notebook and did some figuring.

"There, I think this will allow for the corners and any other cuts you'll have to make. I also wrote down the type of screws you'll need. I put screws along with the nails, I personally believe it makes it a more solid structure."

"Thank you so much for helping me with this. I love this backyard and the only thing holding me back from using it more is this horrible deck. I can't wait to add this to my dream list."

"What's a dream list?" He asked.

"On the fridge you'll see my dream list. I put everything I want to do for my house on there and then tackle the items one at a time." She was proud of her organization.

He chuckled. "How about showing me those lists you created for your sister's case?" Patrick watched for her reaction as he asked.

Laura eagerly agreed. "Of course, that's what you came to see."

She guided him back into the kitchen and down the hallway to the office. When she opened the door, Laura encouraged him to go in first. Patrick walked in but stopped short as he saw the lists written directly on the painted walls. "You do intend to paint these walls, don't you?" He laughed at the sight.

"Of course. I didn't have the fancy whiteboard walls that you do, but I figured this would work." She explained.

"You are an amazing woman, Laura Shepherd. I love it." He stepped forward and looked closely at her lists. She waited patiently for his response.

Finally, he turned to her. "You've thought long and hard about this, haven't you?"

"I don't know about long and hard; it's only been a day or two since I learned that my sister might have big trouble in her life. I feel a deep need to help her in any way I can." She gestured towards the lists on the walls, "I need the answers to these questions. I'm asking for your help."

Patrick put it to her bluntly, "This could mean finding out things you might be sorry about later. It might unearth truths that will hurt you and your family."

"I'm aware of that. I thought about it all night long. Vicky is in danger, but if she's living in the land of denial, it's up to me to try and find out what happened to Randy's first wife. Will you help me?" She asked one more time.

"Yes." Patrick said, "I'll go to my truck and get my briefcase. I copied my files. Put on some more coffee and let's look over your thoughts and compare them with mine. We'll need to develop a plan of attack."

Her laughter made him smile. "It sounds like I should change into my camo clothes and get ready for battle."

"It is similar to a battle plan. We will have to divide and conquer sometimes."

"If we have to play good cop, bad cop, I volunteer to be the good one. I've never done anything like this, so I don't know how much help I can be." Laura shrugged her shoulders.

"Fresh eyes can be a blessing. You'll be fine." He laughed as he went out the front door and soon they were both back in her office. She put the coffee and the rest of the bear claws on her desk.

"You said that you were one of the detectives on the case. How many people were assigned?" Laura asked.

"We had three people looking into Donna's disappearance, I was assigned later in the investigation." He looked at her, anticipation on his face. When she remained quiet, he prompted, "Laura, what's on your mind?"

Without further hesitation, she said, "What do you think you could have done better in the investigation back then?" She went over to the desk but kept her eyes on him. As she took a sip of her cold coffee, she watched Patrick seem to struggle with his thoughts.

Finally, he went over to the list of her questions and pointed to one in particular. "I don't think the daughter was questioned enough. Even though she was only thirteen at the time, she must have known important details about the relationship between her mother and father." Patrick hesitated but continued, "I am not making excuses, but as a new member and a junior part of the investigative team, I feel that I didn't push my ideas enough. Is that what you wanted to know?"

"Why didn't you?"

"Wow, lady, you won't stop, will you?" He turned to stare at her lists on the wall. "This case happened just about the time my wife started into her medical nightmare. I had a hard time keeping my mind focused on anything but her. There were also complications with Donna's disappearance taking place on tribal land. Working between agencies doesn't always allow the communication to be shared efficiently."

"I'm not blaming you, Patrick. I'm just asking questions," she explained. "You said that I might have to face things that could hurt me or my family. Isn't it true for you, too?"

He looked around and with his feet planted firmly on the floor, his hands on his hips, and a stern look on his face, Patrick answered, "Yes."

As they both stood there at an apparent impasse, Laura heard the back door open. Moving quickly, she left the room to greet her granddaughter coming into the kitchen. "Nana, what's up? What are you doing?" Sunny was already at the refrigerator helping herself to a soda.

Laura looked back to the hallway as she heard Patrick moving towards them. "We were talking about the remodel I want to do to this old house. You remember Patrick?"

With a sly grin on her face, Sunshine answered, "Of course I remember this good-looking guy."

"Patrick, I give up! Trying to teach this one some manners is beyond my abilities." She went over and hugged Sunny to her side. "What are you doing here?"

"You wanted my help with painting your office, remember? I was going to start on that today." She smiled innocently.

"Ugh, I do remember that you agreed to help me." Laura looked to Patrick for some help.

He took the hint. "Laura, remember when we looked at your deck? You should use this young lady's super energy and have her start tearing it apart. Sunny, come out here with me and I'll fill you in on what needs to be destroyed."

"Oh, cool! Destruction is what I do best." She turned and flashed her grandmother a wide grin as she followed Patrick. Laura wasn't about to let them go out without her.

Once on the deck, she found Patrick explaining what needed to be done. He was very patient as he described the work and answered the questions Sunny asked.

"This is going to be so cool, Nana. I can't wait to get these old boards out of here." Sunny's enthusiasm was one of the traits that made her so lovable.

"You don't have to start today. I'll get some extra gloves and hammers and then we'll do it together." Laura offered.

"Okay, I get it. You two want to be alone," Sunny interjected with a giggle. "Okay, I'm going home. Let me know when we can get started on this."

"I'll text you, kiddo. I love you," she said to the young girl's back as she disappeared through the sliding glass door. They quickly heard the engine starting on her car.

"Thanks." Laura turned to Patrick.

"I got the message you didn't want her to see the notes on the walls in your office. Why?" he asked as they walked together back into the house.

Once back in the office, she finally responded, "Sunny didn't just happen by. She saw your truck out front, and her natural curiosity got the better of her. She came in to see what we were doing."

"Wow. It's been a long time since I was around a teenager. I've forgotten how tricky they can be." He put his hands on his hips and once again appeared to be studying the notes on the wall.

"You know you do that when you get nervous." She spoke to him.

"What?"

"You plant your feet, put your hands on your hips and frown." She waited for him to respond.

"I frown?" he asked with a confused look on his face. "I don't think I frown."

"Well, you do. I've only been around you for a day or two and that pattern has already been implanted on my brain. It's okay, though, I'm sure I do certain things when I get nervous."

"You do." He didn't elaborate.

"Well...what do I do?" She pushed for him to give more information.

"You laugh. When you get nervous, you giggle." He kept looking at the lists on the wall.

She stifled a giggle.

"See!" He pointed as he turned to face her. "You were ready to laugh, weren't you?"

She swiped at his arm. "Let's get back to this, okay? What do we do next?"

"I think we need to see how many neighbors and coworkers we can find and do some intensive interviews. I'm going to use one of my contacts and see if we can find the daughter. Donna worked at the local casino as a slot attendant."

"She worked at Bucky's?"

"Ah, you know that place?"

"Well, I like to gamble every now and then. I'll go there and see if I can find anyone who worked back then." Laura volunteered. "Is that where Donna disappeared from?"

"Yes, it was a busy holiday weekend when she vanished, and the employees all had to park on that lot down below. Her car was found there after she was reported missing."

"Don't they give the workers a ride from the casino? Wouldn't you have interviewed the shuttle driver? What did they have to say back then?"

"Good questions. I think what we should do is start from scratch. I know that people's memories will have faded, but sometimes you can still gain new information with a fresh approach. Your sister and her husband work at the college. Why don't you go there, and I'll handle the casino." He suggested.

"I have a better idea. I'll go to the college around lunchtime to see if I can catch some of the maintenance crew who work with Randy to talk with them and then I can meet you at the casino later. It'll give me a chance to see you in action." She waited for his reaction.

He stood up. "Okay, we'll meet tonight around 9:00." The knowing grin on his face showed that he knew she was exerting her independence in this investigation. On his way out, Patrick grabbed his hat. "See you at the casino."

Laura looked at the clock and hurried to change her blouse and jeans. If she hurried, she would get to the college just in time for lunch for most of the employees. Driving down the street gave her time to think of what she was going to say to the maintenance workers. She giggled but stopped when she realized Patrick had been right about her nervous habit.

The parking lot was full, but she finally found a space. As she hurried to the campus cafeteria, Laura tried to gather her thoughts about how to gain some valuable information. Shrugging her shoulders, Laura entered and looked for the guys from maintenance. There were several of them sitting at a table in the back. As she headed their way, Laura was thinking about her approach, but fate was on her side. She was happy to see a familiar face. "Verne!" She spoke and sat down at the table next to her friend. "I almost forgot you worked here at the college."

"Laura, nice to see you! What are you doing here?" He grinned.

"Oh, I was just thinking about enrolling in another class but decided to see what was on the menu for lunch first." She answered with the first thing that she could think of as a reason for her visit to the campus but realized it might be a good idea to look at the class schedule after all. She had always believed that education was the key to one's future.

Verne turned to introduce her to the others at the table as she sat down next to him. "This is Laura Shepherd. She was our neighbor for a little while before she bought that fixer-upper close to downtown. Trisha misses you. How's that remodel going?"

She smiled and spoke proudly. "I can honestly say I'm truly enjoying the work. I'm sure that I can't do things as well as you all can, but everything seems to be coming out okay. I thought you would be retired by now."

"I think I'm getting close. Trisha wants me to slow down and maybe do some traveling."

"How long have you worked at the college?" Hope soared as she waited for his answer.

"Can you believe, I'm very close to twenty years here."

"Wow, Verne, that makes you as old as dirt." One of the coworkers teased him.

"Not quite, our fearless leader is older than me and taking care of all of you has given him all those gray hairs."

"Yeah, but Randy can sit back now and watch all of us sweat while we do all the hard work." The guys were having fun with the discussion.

"Has Randy always been the director?" She tried to dig for information about the relationship between Verne and Randy.

"He's been my boss for at least ten years now, but we worked side-by-side at the beginning. I'm ready to retire, but I don't think he's anywhere near to it."

"You two have been through a lot, huh?" She had to restrain herself from going directly to the point.

Verne kept eating his lunch. "We started here when this college was very small and easy to take care of. It was good work even though there were only five of us back then. Now I have to put up with all these jokers." They all laughed.

She had to restrain her excitement. "Wow! I bet you two had to do a lot of repairs on your own."

"Yeah, Randy went through a rough patch back then and I was left on my own sometimes, but that's how I learned how to handle things I wouldn't normally do."

"Oh, what happened?" She hoped her enthusiasm wasn't showing.

"Well, you didn't live here back then but it was huge local news. His first wife disappeared mysteriously."

A group exclamation came from the employees sitting around the table. "Wow! That's rough, what happened?" One of them asked.

"She just disappeared and to this day has never been found. It was pretty hard on him, that's why I had to carry most of the work. I didn't mind. I know he would have done it for me if the situation had been reversed."

Suddenly the atmosphere at the table became more serious as she felt hands on her shoulders. A shiver went up her spine as Laura realized it was Randy. All eyes were looking above her head.

"Laura, what are you doing here?" His voice was calm, but she sensed he was unhappy to see her with his workers.

"Randy," She spoke and at the same time moved away from his touch while turning to look at him. "I was talking with my old neighbor, Verne."

He moved over to the other side of the table and took the only empty chair. "I think these guys are about ready to go back to work, aren't you?" His comments set the workers in motion as they stood and cleaned up the lunch mess, except for Verne, who took his time to pack the remainder of his lunch back into his bag. He slowly stood up and addressed Laura, "Great to see you again. Give Trisha a call. She'd love to hear from you." He saluted Randy and left just the two of them at the table.

She put on a brave face as she too stood up, ready to leave. "See you later."

"Wait a minute." His voice sounded cold. "I know your sister has talked with you about our problems, but I just want to reassure you, we're fine. You don't need to worry." The smile on his face was more menacing than friendly.

"That's exactly what I told her." She turned and walked away. Her feet wanted to run, but Laura maintained her composure all the way across the room and out the door. Once in her car, she finally let out her breath.

T hree

With shaking hands, Laura started her car and slowly worked her way out of the crowded parking lot. Her thoughts were chaotic as she drove the short distance back to her home. She still had several hours before meeting Patrick, and nothing helped to calm her mind more than some good, honest hard work. Donning her work clothes, Laura grabbed her hammer and gloves and stepped out onto her back deck.

With her mind still reeling from the interaction with her brother-in-law, Laura kneeled at the end of the deck and using the claw end of her hammer, started pulling at the nails holding the boards to her deck. It was much harder than she thought it was going to be but, determined to work out her frustrations, she kept at it.

A male voice startled her and Laura raised her hammer.

"Whoa! I didn't mean to scare you. Mother, what in hell are you doing?" Josh took a few steps back out of her reach.

Trying hard to regain her composure and stop her beating heart, Laura diverted the conversation, "I'm finally doing something about this old deck. Why don't you grab that crowbar from the garage and help me?" She stood and stretched her achy back muscles.

"Why don't you have your new boyfriend help you?" Josh laughed at the expression on his mother's face as he teased her.

"That daughter of yours has a vivid imagination."

"How come she's my daughter and not your beloved Sunny when she acts like a brat?" He stood there waiting for his mother to answer his question. "So, who's the new man in your life?"

"Go and get that crowbar, son." She had no intention of getting into this topic right now.

Josh came back with the tool and as they worked together, she was pleased with their progress. His muscle power was what had been needed to get the old, damaged wood up from the frame of the deck. Finally, they had the entire back section cleared.

"You're going to need to put something there to get into your back door." Josh pointed out the obvious.

"I have some cinder blocks over there. Let's get them and make a temporary stairway."

"I'll get the blocks. You start to stack this old wood close to the gate. I can haul the boards in my truck and get rid of them at the dump on my way home."

"I'll just carry them to your truck, no sense in lifting them twice." She picked up several boards and carefully made her way out of the back yard up to his truck. After a few more trips, Laura hollered at Josh. "Hey, let's go in and get something to drink. I'm beat." They'd been working for several hours, and she still had to clean up to meet Patrick at the casino.

"Try this." Josh pointed to the temporary steps he'd created.

Laura moved over the framework of the deck and stepped on the blocks. "This will do until I can get the new decking down. Thanks, son."

They sat in the kitchen and shared a glass of cold iced tea. "Thanks for your help. I wouldn't have gotten all that done without you."

"It'll cost you." He raised his glass to sip the sweet tea.

"I'm sure it will." She agreed.

"You seem a little uptight. What's going on?" Josh asked.

"Nothing's going on, I'm just working hard on this house." She tried to convince him.

"Mother, I know your moods and this one says you're worried about something. Come on, give." He looked straight at her, waiting for an answer. "I scared you half to death when I first walked up. You were ready to hit me with your hammer!"

"Son, I'm not ready to talk about it yet." She tried to put him off.

"Mom! Sunny has met the man and I think I have a right to know something about him. I worry about you."

"Okay, okay. He's just someone I'm consulting with about the deck. He's a retired detective who does home remodeling on the side." She hoped her shortened version would satisfy her son.

"So, no romantic interest, huh?" he prodded.

"Oh, my God, no! Once in a lifetime is enough." She protested. "Josh, if he was important, I'd make sure you met him, but it's not anything like that. He's just helping me remodel the deck."

The look on his face showed that her son was still not believing her story. He stood up, ready to leave. She joined him as they walked to the side kitchen door. "Hey, what are you doing home in the middle of the day?"

"I just took a day off. I needed some time away from that place. I had a job interview with a new company, and I think I might get it." Josh reluctantly shared his news.

"I know you've been unhappy there. Maybe this will work out and give you a fresh start. Thanks for helping me." She reached up and gave him a peck on his cheek. "You're a good son."

"You be careful," he warned.

"What do you mean?" For a minute Laura thought he was talking about the investigation into Randy's past.

"I mean with the new handyman. You're so trusting. I don't want to see someone taking advantage of you." He kissed her in return and let the door shut behind him.

Laura checked the time on the kitchen clock and saw she had time for a bath. She turned to lock the back door before going to clean up. Her son was right about her being a trusting sort of person, but the exchange with Randy spooked her.

Just as she was taking off her clothes, her cell phone rang. "Laura?" She recognized Verne's voice.

"Verne. What's up?"

"I just figured out that Randy and your sister are married now." His gravelly voice gave her no hint as to his meaning.

"Yes, they've been married about ten years. I thought you knew that." Her senses were alert.

"Well, I guess I knew that, but it didn't really sink in until he put his hands on your shoulders. That kinda threw me."

She attempted a small giggle. "Yeah, he's my brother-in-law, good ole Randy."

"He came and found me after you left. He was asking a whole bunch of questions about why you were here at the college." Verne hesitated but continued, "I just thought it was weird. I've known Randy a long time, but lately he's just been acting kind of strange. Just thought you should know."

"Well, Verne, I don't think there's any need for worry, but thanks for your concern. I'll give Trisha a call soon." She tried to make light of the situation, but her nerves were on full alert.

Checking the time once again, Laura realized she had plenty of time before cleaning up and meeting Patrick. As she went down the hallway past her office, she saw the notes on the walls. Taking out her phone, she snapped pictures of all the notes. Grabbing the primer paint can sitting on the floor, Laura decided that she shouldn't leave these notes up where anyone could read them. With Randy's menacing behavior, she was feeling a little threatened, even in her own home.

It took her over an hour to put enough paint on the walls to completely cover the notes. As soon as she finished all the area, Laura rested for a moment and then touched up some spaces where the marker pen was still showing through. Standing back, finally satisfied, Laura put the lid on the paint and cleaned up her brushes and rollers. With all the physical work she'd done so far today, her muscles were a bit achy.

She took her time bathing. The hot water felt good on her sore back and arms. She combed out her hair and did her best to style the wild red curls. The time on her phone indicated she had plenty of time to eat dinner and then meet Patrick at Bucky's Casino.

Before leaving her house, Laura made sure each door was locked. Normally she wouldn't have made that much effort, as living in this small town had always felt very safe. With the investigation underway and Randy alerted, she wasn't about to take any chances with her safety. As she passed the mirror in her front room, Laura adjusted her hair one last time and then admonished herself. I'm not out to impress anyone, she thought firmly.

She checked the rear-view mirror several times on the way to the casino. "Damn!" Laura exclaimed as she realized that the encounter with Randy had left her feeling vulnerable. Determined to change that, she vowed to move forward and search for the truth.

The hotel had originally been owned by a national chain on the reservation, but the tribe eventually bought the property and now ran the hotel resort and casino on their own. She made the left turn and headed up the steep, short drive to the top of the hill to Bucky's. The view was beautiful as she parked her car. The city lights were popping up all over and she took a moment to appreciate her life in this little northern Arizona city.

She was able to find a parking spot near the entrance, and chose the lower-level door, not knowing where she might find Patrick. As she walked around that ground floor, Laura found the casino busy with laughing patrons playing the noisy machines. Even in the middle of the week, it seemed busy with activity. Not finding Patrick, she took the steps up to the second level and walked around looking for him.

He wasn't at the blackjack tables nor at any of the machines around the perimeter of this floor, so she started up the stairs to the third and final floor. As she took the last step, Laura saw Patrick sitting at the bar talking with people on chairs nearby. His now familiar black cowboy hat was firmly planted on his head and she noticed his charming smile as he laughed at something the woman on his right said to him.

Taking a deep reassuring breath, Laura walked up to the bar and greeted him. "Patrick, have you been waiting long?"

He stood and took his hat off to speak to her. "No, I've just been here long enough to lose the farm."

The woman gave out a loud, raucous laugh. "You've barely put in any money. Don't believe him, honey. He hasn't even lost the price of a beer." She took a big gulp of her drink and kept punching the buttons on her machine.

Laura looked from her to Patrick but then burst out laughing, too. "Well, I'm glad we still have some money in the bank."

"What are you having to drink?" He didn't sit back down, but instead offered Laura his stool. "Mary." He called to the smiling bartender.

"Patrick, what do you need now?" She teased in a familiar way. "Mary, this is Laura." He turned to Laura, "What would you like to drink?"

"Well, how about a glass of white wine. I can have one and still drive home."

Mary smiled, "Hi, nice to meet you. I have a good chardonnay you might like." She moved down the bar to pour the drink.

"You come here often?" As soon as she said it, Laura laughed, "My, that sounds like a bad opening line, doesn't it?"

Patrick's deep resonant laughter was addicting, and they enjoyed a fun moment. "I can assure you, I've never used that one."

By that time, the bartender returned with her drink and one for Patrick, a popular beer with a lime. "Do you want to run a tab?"

"No, I think we'll just have these for now. Thanks, Mary." As the man beside Laura got up to leave, he offered his stool to Patrick.

"This one-armed bandit has taken enough of my dough. It's all yours if you want it."

"Thanks, is it okay with you to stay here?" Patrick asked Laura.

She nodded her head to agree. "I'm not sure I know how to play these machines."

"Oh, they're not difficult, just put your money in and they'll take it." Showing the same welcoming smile, Mary came back just in time to overhear Laura's remark.

"Mary's been here for quite a while now, haven't you?" Patrick prompted.

"Too long, if you ask me." She was busy preparing drinks and greeting customers as she talked. "Patrick, I think I've been here longer than you were on the sheriff's team. I just passed twenty years behind this bar."

"Oh, I think that's amazing." Laura added her comment.

"I'll have you both know I've been in law enforcement for almost thirty years. So there!" Patrick put some money into the machine in front of him and handed Laura a hundred-dollar bill.

"What am I supposed to do with this?" Laura was surprised by his gesture.

"Don't look a gift horse in the mouth, honey. Put it in that machine and win a big jackpot!" Mary's laughter could be heard as she went to help other customers with their drink orders.

Patrick leaned over to whisper to Laura. "She could be a great source of information, but it may take some time. Please just put the money in and play slowly."

"Oh, I get it! I'm new at this, so you'll have to forgive me if I don't catch on right away." She put the money in and selected one of the poker games.

They both played for a while when Patrick finally asked, "How did it go at the college? Did you learn anything that might help?"

She tried to hide behind a giggle, but remembering his comments from earlier, Laura decided to answer honestly. "I had a rather strange run-in with my brother-in-law."

Immediately Patrick was attentive. "Laura, what happened? He didn't do anything to you, did he? You weren't harmed, were you?"

"No, no. I went to the college at lunch time. I figured I could talk with some of the guys who work with Randy, you know he's the supervisor in the maintenance department. Well, I ran into my former neighbor Verne. I sat down at their table where several employees were eating lunch."

He interrupted her, "I should have gone with you. You've never done anything like this. It could get dangerous."

"Whoa, whoa. I put my big girl panties on today and I can handle myself." She turned her attention back to the game she was playing.

For a few anxious moments, they both concentrated their attention away from each other. Mary came over, unaware of the tension between Patrick and Laura. "Hey, this is supposed to be fun. You two look very serious. You're going to scare away my other customers."

As Laura raised her head to apologize, she saw that they were the only two people at the bar. Seeing the huge smile on the bartender's face, she realized Mary was teasing them. "Well, it looks like we've already succeeded in running your business in the ground."

"I think that calls for another drink." Before Laura could protest, Patrick added, "We'll share a ride if we need to and come back tomorrow for our cars."

"Oh, what the hell! Give me another wine."

As Mary walked to the cooler at the other end of the bar, Patrick leaned over and spoke quietly. "I'm sorry. I didn't mean to come across as a caveman. Taking care of my wife for so long has obviously strengthened my protective instincts. I'll work on it."

"Thank you. I, too, can be a bit over the top when it comes to my independence. I was just fifteen when I got married."

"Wow, that is young!"

"Before you ask, I wasn't pregnant. I've always been an old soul, even at that tender age. When I met Carl, well, I thought he was the one I wanted to be with for the rest of my life. Funny how things work out, huh?"

Mary came back to talk. "Patrick, don't you miss working after all those years with the sheriff's office? You must wish for the excitement of a good murder investigation." She laughed.

"You are too much, Mary. I am so busy with my remodeling business that I wouldn't have time to solve any crime right now, let alone a good murder, as you call it." A happy grin crossed over his face. "I'll have you know that I am a state-certified private investigator if I really wanted to jump back into solving crimes."

Laura interjected, "So, you solved all the murders you investigated over those thirty years?" She noticed the glimmer in his eyes as he realized the opening she had just given him.

"As a matter of fact, there are exactly four cases that I never solved. Mary, you might remember the one involving Donna Bell, the slot attendant who worked here."

"Oh, yeah, but she wasn't murdered, she just disappeared."

"It was so long ago. I doubt that you remember anything about it." He dared the friendly bartender.

"I remember plenty, but wait..." Mary yelled across the floor, "Rick! Can you come over here?"

They all watched as Rick, the slot attendant, walked over to the bar. "What's up?"

"This is Patrick and Laura." Mary introduced them.

"It's nice to see you. Are you two ready to win a jackpot?" Rick asked.

"Rick, they have some questions." Mary stated. "What do you remember about the slot attendant, Donna Bell?"

For a moment he didn't speak, but soon Rick turned to them, "Donna was a great person. I enjoyed working with her. It was a very long time ago when I knew her."

"Then you did know Donna?" Patrick asked.

"Sure, I'm not so old and senile yet." Rick joked. "I am ready to retire, but working here is good money and it's hard to give it up."

"What can you tell us about her disappearance?" Laura asked.

"Oh, wow, it was so long ago. If I remember right, Donna caught the shuttle to the parking lot below, but she disappeared and was never seen again."

"Oh my God, what did you all do?" Laura asked.

"Well, the sheriff's department and tribal police were called in, of course. It was a busy weekend with the town full of people, so we didn't get a lot of information until a few days later." Mary added.

"We were all questioned, you know, the ones in her department. I don't think all the employees knew that she'd been reported missing, just the ones who worked with her that night," Rick added. "Did you ever find her?" he asked Patrick.

"No, it's like she just disappeared off the face of the earth. One of the theories we were leaning towards was that she had another man on the side and just left everything behind."

"You know, now that you mention it, Donna was unhappy with her husband. All I ever heard was what a jerk he was to her." Rick added.

"Really? Did you know the man she was seeing?" Laura asked.

Before Rick could answer, he received a notification in his earpiece that a jackpot needed to be paid on the lower floor. "I'll be back in a minute."

"Did you know Donna was seeing another man?" Patrick asked Mary.

"Well, you know how girls talk. She never mentioned the other man by name, but I could tell she thought she was really in love. Her husband was always gone, and Donna just needed some attention. I never thought she would leave though; you know she had a teenage daughter. I can't imagine a woman leaving her child without at least contacting her or even taking her along." Mary saw a customer trying to get her attention and moved to help him.

"You know, my son and my sister talk frequently, and Josh told me the same thing about Randy. He says that Vicky complains that he's away from home a lot and she's left alone." Laura reflected on the similarity of the two marriages. "I wonder what it is that he's doing that keeps him away?"

"Maybe it's time to follow Randy for a few days," Patrick thought aloud. "I don't mean you should do this. It might be too dangerous as he seems upset with you right now."

"Why don't we do it together? I think it would be interesting to observe his routines and behavior." She suggested. Laura kept playing the poker game during their talk.

"That sounds great. We'll get some details figured out and plan it. How about another drink? We'll play a bit more and then call for an Uber." Patrick waved at Mary.

I should refuse, Laura thought for a moment, but she found herself enjoying time with him. She needed his help to find out what Randy was capable of and to protect her sister, but she hadn't expected to like this man sitting next to her.

"Here you are." Mary placed their drinks on fresh napkins but before leaving, added, "I wonder what ever happened to Donna's daughter. Kids can be affected the rest of their lives by something like that."

As she walked away, Patrick spoke. "I've got someone tracking the daughter down. Hopefully we can find and interview her. Mary's probably right, having your mother disappear would definitely impact your life. When my wife died, our kids were in their twenties, but it was hard on them both."

"It had to have been hard on all of you." Laura said.

Before Patrick could respond, the machine she was playing on suddenly froze and bells started going off. "What's happening?" Laura asked.

Mary rushed over and she and Patrick started laughing. "You just hit the royal flush! You won a thousand dollars." He put his arm around her shoulders and pulled her closer in a big hug.

"I'll call Rick to come and pay you!" Mary reached for a walkie-talkie to announce the jackpot. Several people wandered over to see how much she won.

"Oh, my goodness. How lucky! I really don't play poker much at all. This is fun!" Laura beamed.

About that time, Rick came up the stairs. With a big smile on his face, he congratulated Laura. "Aren't you the lucky one?" He pulled out the bills to pay her.

"Oh, no, this is Patrick's money. You should be paying it to him." She protested.

"Sorry, but I have to pay it to you, so hold out your hand. The cameras see all and you're the one sitting in front of this bad boy. What you do with it after I put this money in your hand is your business." With a big grin, Rick carefully counted out ten one-hundred-dollar bills into her open hand. She looked at Patrick, who nodded his head.

"Here you are. Thank you so much!" Laura handed Rick one of the bills.

"Are you sure?" If his grin could get any bigger, it just did.

"Yes, Rick, we thank you for the money and the information." Patrick confirmed.

"Hey, I remembered something else about that day. Donna's husband came into the casino and they were having a rather heated discussion. I couldn't hear what was being said, but you could tell that it wasn't friendly." Rick supplied further information. "Randy left, Donna went on a break. I saw her sitting with one of her best friends here, a cashier. She doesn't work here anymore but still lives in Prescott. You might want to talk with her. Her name is Debbie Ortega."

"You know Patrick was a detective with the sheriff's department, don't you?" Mary told Rick and turned to Patrick, "You would have spoken with Debbie, wouldn't you?"

"I'll have to look over my notes. I don't remember everything from the investigation. Like you all have said, it was a long time ago." His answer surprised Laura, but she didn't let it show. "Hey, thanks, Rick, for the information and especially for all of this." Patrick fanned the bills Laura had put in his hand.

"I think it's time for us to go, while we're still winners." Laura stood up.

"I agree. Mary, Rick, thanks for everything. It's been fun." He put his hand in the small of her back as they walked towards the stairs. Step by step they went down until they were on the second floor. Patrick asked the security officer standing at the railing to call them a ride.

"Let's go outside and wait on the bench."

The night air and silence settled nicely on her shoulders. Laura loved sitting on her back deck listening to the crickets and a few barks from the neighborhood dogs. The constant noise of the casino wasn't an environment she would enjoy on a regular basis. Patrick sat down. She joined him as they waited for their Uber driver.

"Here, I want you to take this money. You won it."

"Absolutely not! It was yours from the start. You would have to take the loss so why not take the winnings," she protested.

"I'm beginning to learn you have a stubborn streak a mile long." He stuffed the money back into his front pocket.

Laura just laughed, "I've been told that more than once."

Just then a car pulled up and as they got in, Patrick gave her address to the driver. "We'll drop you off first. I'll call another Uber in the morning, and we'll go back and get our vehicles."

As the Uber driver pulled up in front of her house, Laura immediately became concerned. It appeared that every light in the house was turned on, blazing through the windows. Patrick noticed her reaction and turned to see the same sight. "What is it? Why are the lights on?"

Thinking about her negative interaction with Randy and their current investigation, Laura started to jump from the car as soon as it stopped, but Patrick pulled her back. "Stay here!" His voice was laced with fear as he spoke to her.

"Turn off the lights," he ordered the driver.

Patrick got out of the car and pulled a gun from the back of his pants and slowly crept up the lawn to the front door. "Wait, Patrick, Sunny's car is in the drive." Laura was right behind him by then and together they made their way to the porch.

Suddenly the front door was flung open, and her granddaughter ran out. "Nana! Patrick! I'm so glad you guys are here." She ran into Laura's open arms, tears streaming down her face.

Four

"Are you alright?" Both Patrick and Laura voiced their concern at the same time.

"I'm fine now that you're here. I came over and when I found you weren't home, I decided to come in, have a snack and wait. I was in the living room watching TV when I heard a huge noise at the back of the house. It was so loud but when I looked out, I couldn't see anything. As I was staring at the back yard, I saw a person, a man I think, running from the deck. He was wearing a hoodie, so I couldn't see any details."

Patrick immediately started to the back door but not before turning off the lights on his way to the kitchen and back deck. "Careful! There's no deck out there." Her words stopped him just in time. "When did you do that?" He turned back to ask.

"My son came over today and together we almost have the entire deck destroyed. We did put some cinder blocks down for steps."

Before looking down, Patrick ordered them to stay quiet and stay there. He looked down, trying to see the blocks before carefully stepping down. His gun was still in his hand and soon Patrick was out of their sight. Sunny and Laura had turned out the other lights in the house and stood in the dark, peering out, listening for Patrick's footsteps and any other sounds that would indicate what was going on during his search.

There was a slight breeze in the night air, but other than the sound of the wind rustling through the trees surrounding her large yard, they heard nothing. The urge to call Patrick's name was strong but Laura knew it wouldn't help the situation, and she trusted his skills.

"Nana," Sunny's whispered voice was close. "I'm glad he's here. This was so scary. Should we call the sheriff?"

"Definitely." Laura dialed the emergency number and requested assistance. Once she completed her call, she asked, "Sunny, what exactly did you hear?"

"I was in the living room eating some of that fantastic chocolate cake. I was just about to turn on the TV when I thought I heard you coming home. I got up and looked out the front window and that's when I heard the huge crash from the back of the house."

"What did it sound like? I mean, can you think carefully about the actual sound to figure out what it was?"

"It wasn't a gunshot or anything like that. It was more like a thud...wait, there was the noise like glass breaking. Now that I think of it, it sounded like someone threw something like a rock at a window." Sunny concluded.

"She's right." Patrick's voice startled them both.

"What did you find out?" Laura asked.

"One of those cinder blocks that you used for the steps was missing. I had to use the flashlight on my phone, but the only thing I could do was walk around the back of your place. Someone tried to throw that block through the window in your bedroom. Those blinds you have on the inside of your bedroom window successfully stopped it from coming all the way into the room."

"Why would someone do something like that? My Nana wouldn't hurt a flea." Sunny hugged her grandmother.

Their eyes met over Sunny's head and the message was clear between them. "Are the sheriffs on their way?" He asked.

"Yes. I have a piece of plywood in the garage. Maybe it'll be big enough to cover up the window until morning."

"Let's wait for the sheriff. I can put it up after they inspect the damage."

"Patrick, do you want some of Nana's cake? It's really, really good." Sunny asked with the innocence of her young age.

"Sure. We can wait for the sheriff with some great chocolate cake." Patrick tried to calm himself and the others with the lighthearted banter.

They had not waited long when the doorbell rang. Patrick moved to answer the door and greeted an officer he knew. After introducing Laura and Sunny to the detective, he said, "You two stay in here. We'll be right back."

Laura would have wanted to hear the conversation between the two men, but understanding that Sunny needed her for comfort, she reluctantly agreed and nodded her head. "Are you alright?" She asked her granddaughter.

"Nana, I'm fine. Are you going to finally tell me what's going on? Is this related to Uncle Randy and his problems?"

With a deep sigh, Laura decided to share some information. "Sunny, you must keep all of this to yourself. Patrick and I have just started investigating and don't have any real details yet, just suspicions. What's happened here tonight could be an indication that things might get dangerous."

"Now you're scaring me."

"You should be concerned." Patrick's voice was heard from the kitchen as he and the detective came back into the house. "This was intended to be a warning. Next time it could be a lot more serious."

"What did you find?" Laura asked.

The young officer from the sheriff's department answered, "They threw the block, but if they really wanted to, it would have penetrated that window. It was meant to do what it did, scare you."

The officer turned to shake Patrick's hand as they crossed to the front door. "Ladies, I'll be in touch. Patrick, we'll talk again."

"Ready to put up that plywood?" She asked.

"Bring your flashlight and I'll put it up. You can help me. Sunny, you wait in here."

Together they went and grabbed everything necessary to board up the broken window. As they walked around the house, Laura finally spoke the thoughts whirling around in her head. "Do you think it was Randy?"

"Do you?"

"I'd like to think that it was just some kid being stupid, but with everything going on now, I'd say it could be possible." Her words were tinged with sadness.

They worked together and Patrick made sure the window was covered completely. As they walked to the back door, he turned to her. "Laura, I think I'll spend the night here tonight."

She opened her mouth to protest but the words wouldn't come as Laura realized she was shaking with fear. As they came into the kitchen, Sunny was waiting for them. "Is it taken care of? Is my Nana going to be safe?"

"Yes, I'm going to stay here all night. Why don't you stay, too?" Patrick proposed, "You can be our chaperone. We wouldn't want the neighbors to talk." His easy grin made Sunny smile and she joined in with his teasing.

"Nana does have a wild streak and the neighbors are already talking."

"Sunny!" She shrugged with defeat. "Call your dad and tell him you're staying here." As an afterthought, she added, "Do not tell him anything about Patrick staying or about the broken window! I don't need any of his comments tonight."

She went to the guest room to gather an extra pillow and some blankets. "Sunny, you get the couch. Patrick, I'll show you where you can sleep. I don't know about you, but I'm beat and ready for bed."

Laura went about locking the doors and as she grabbed a bottle of water for herself and Patrick, she took a moment to stand in the darkened kitchen and gather her thoughts. What a mess this is becoming, she thought. Could Randy be a man capable of murder? Could he be responsible for the damage to her house? Am I putting Sunny in danger? Suddenly she realized Patrick was standing at the doorway, watching her.

"Are you alright? Don't overthink this, Laura. We'll figure things out, I promise. You and Sunny will be safe."

"I'm going to hold you to that promise, Patrick."

She left the room and once down the hall, closed her bedroom door. Laura didn't turn on a light but sat on the edge of her bed. Her body started shaking and she wrapped her arms around her middle to stop the tremors. I've got to get Vicky away from that man. She's got to listen to reason. Before she could get undressed, there was a firm knock on the door.

"Laura." His voice penetrated the solid wood door as he opened it slowly. "Are you decent?"

"Yes, what's wrong?"

"I'm going to stay in here tonight." Once he saw the look of shock on her face, he clarified, "I mean alone. You are going to sleep in the guest room. If there's going to be any harm done, I'll be here waiting to reciprocate." He pulled his gun out and placed it on the stand beside the bed.

"I'll just grab my pajamas."

"What? You're not going to fight me on this?" Patrick challenged.

She stopped, put her hands on her hips and faced him. "Under normal conditions, I would be making the decisions in my own home, but with everything that's happened and my granddaughter in the front room, I'll allow you to think you're in charge, at least for tonight." With that she shut the door firmly behind her. His laughter followed her down the hall and into the guest room. She slammed that door too, but it didn't give her the satisfaction she thought it would.

Sleep evaded her for what seemed like hours, but finally Laura found herself giving in to the slumber that she needed. The sun would normally have been shining in her eyes if she'd been in her own room, but as Laura rolled over to wake up, the memories from last night came flooding in her mind. She remembered her bedroom window was covered up and Patrick was lying in her bed. Putting those thoughts out of her mind, Laura dressed in a hurry and as she headed to the kitchen, heard Patrick and Sunny talking. The smell of coffee perked up her senses as she reached for her favorite cup.

"Morning, Nana. Did you get some sleep?"

"I did, even though I didn't think I would when I went to bed last night. How about you?" Laura avoided meeting Patrick's gaze.

"I'm a good couch sleeper, so I did fine."

Laura finally looked to Patrick and asked, "Did you sleep okay?"

"Yes. I'm going to inspect outside." He stood up.

"Are you looking for evidence?" Sunny probed.

"As a matter of fact, I am."

"Can I come along? I've never met a detective before, and it would be fun to see what you do." Sunny asked.

"Sure, if your grandmother doesn't mind." He looked for approval.

"When do you have to be in class? If you have time, go ahead, but don't miss school, young lady."

"Nana!" She followed Patrick out the back door into the beautiful sunshine of a spring morning. "Sometimes she treats me like a little girl. I know she only wants the best for me, but..."

Patrick just laughed. "She does mean well, but you know that, don't you?"

"Yes. What are we looking for?" She was careful to step in his footprints and follow closely behind him.

"I'm looking for tracks and anything else that might give me a clue as to the identity of the intruder." He walked carefully, looking all around.

"Patrick, look here." She pointed to a piece of fabric stuck on one of the deck railings.

"Good job!" He studied the small patch of fabric that was stuck on a nail. As he looked closely, he noticed a dark stain on the ground below. "It looks like he might have caught his pant leg and even got a nasty scratch on his leg." Patrick bent down to carefully examine the spot on the ground. "See this, it might be a bit of blood."

"Want me to get something to put it in?" Sunny was excited to help.

"Yes, go get a plastic baggie. Oh, and bring a big trash bag."

As the morning progressed, Patrick and Sunny found a few more footprints but nothing more. He carefully put the trash bag over the cinder block and took it to the front porch. "Do you think you can get fingerprints from that?" Laura asked.

"It's worth a try, but I have my doubts. They've come a long way in the area of forensic evidence since I retired. Those guys are total experts in their field. Do you think Sunny can drop us off at the casino to get our cars? I promised a client that I'd start their job today."

With a lot of effort, they were soon piled into Sunny's little car. She raced down the street, giggling the whole time. "Patrick, you're too big for my car. Look, Nana, his head is hitting the top." Sunny's giggles echoed through the car during the short ride to the casino. Once they were dropped off, Laura and Patrick turned to get in their own vehicles. Before Patrick got into his truck, he said, "Laura, please be careful, but most of all, observant. I'll call later."

A few steps from her, Patrick turned to speak an afterthought. "I know you're worried, as well you should be, but please don't try doing anything on your own that might put you in harm's way."

The look on her face confirmed for Patrick that Laura was planning her next move. He came back and got right in her face, "Shall I share a statistic with you in order to convince you to be safe?"

When she didn't reply, he stated it anyway. "Over 75% of murder victims know their killer! Think about that before you decide to do something not so smart!"

"I get it! I'm not in this alone and with my sister and now Sunny affected by our investigation, I will NOT make any stupid decisions, Mr. Patrick Dickson." Calming down a bit, she added, "I thank you for caring, but have a little faith in me."

With a soothing voice, he spoke, "Laura, we've just begun to know each other, and you have no reason to trust me, but please believe me, I am just looking out for your safety. I've seen the worst side of humanity for over thirty years, and I don't want you to become some sick bastard's next victim."

"I'll be safe, I promise. Go, meet your client. Call me later if you want. I've got to call my handyman and get that window replaced." With that, she started to get into her car.

"See ya!" He strode across the parking lot to his truck. She watched him but he never turned around.

Before starting her car, Laura called her handyman and was assured that he could handle the glass replacement without her. He was a trusted friend and had a key to her house. Once that was settled, she headed to her old neighborhood. Her mind was set on gaining information that would open new clues as to what happened to Randy's first wife and keep her sister safe.

As Laura pulled into the driveway of her former neighbor, she saw Trisha working in the front yard. She put on a smile and greeted her with affection. "Trisha, you shouldn't be doing this hard work by yourself."

"I don't have to if some nice young woman comes along to help me." She got up on her knees and

Laura bent down to give her a friendly hug. "It's been too long. Good to see you. Verne said you came to visit at the college."

"I did. I wanted to sign up for a class and found him and his crew in the dining room. It was fun to talk to them."

Trisha put out her hand for help and together they got her to her feet. "Let's go and have a cup of coffee and catch up on all the gossip. I made some apple crisp."

"Your apple crisp is the best. You don't have to say any more. I'm sold." Together the two women walked up the steps and into the older house.

Once in the kitchen, Trisha filled two cups of coffee and set the dessert on the table between them. "Help yourself and tell me what's going on in your life."

They talked for a while catching up on family news but finally Laura approached the subject on her mind. "Trisha, do you remember Randy's first wife?"

"I met her a time or two at some of those office parties. She seemed like a nice person. I didn't really like her husband, though."

"Why?" It was a simple question.

Trisha looked her in the eye at that point. "You tell me. Your sister is now married to him. What do you think?"

It was uncomfortable to have the tables turned, but Laura answered honestly. "This is just between us girls, isn't it?" Once she saw the nod of her friend's head, she continued, "I don't dislike Randy, but he is, how can I say this, he runs hot and cold.

Sometimes he's real friendly and other times he's distant and cold."

"A real Jekyll and Hyde, huh?"

"Wow, I guess you could say that. My sister loves him and for her sake, I try to ignore his sometimes-rude behavior. What I really hate is how demeaning he can be."

"Well, he did the same thing to Donna, his first wife. He even treated her badly in front of other people at those office parties. That's where I met him. We didn't socialize with them outside of the college." Trisha pushed the pan of apple crisp over to Laura. "Help yourself to some more."

"I've missed your desserts. I'm not much of a cook, as you might remember." She laughed as she took another generous portion of the sweet treat.

"Oh, baloney! I'll never forget that quiche dish you brought to our neighborhood get-togethers. I think I even asked you for the recipe and never got it." Trisha teased.

"That's because I was embarrassed to tell you that it was made with Spam. Not everyone likes that canned meat, you know."

"Hell, I was raised on that stuff. We were poor and when Verne and I first got married, we didn't have much either. I used to fry it and make him sandwiches to take to work for lunch."

They laughed together and sat in a comfortable silence for a little while. Finally, Laura stood up, "Trisha, I'm sorry it's been so long. I promise our next visit will be sooner."

At the door, Trisha gave her a hug, but before Laura got too many steps away, Trisha spoke. "You know, there was something that I've never forgotten about that man." She rubbed her chin.

Laura slowly came back to listen. Her instincts about danger came to the forefront while waiting for Trisha to finish her thoughts.

"Just after his wife disappeared, Randy asked my Verne to come and help him at their house. I thought he might be needing someone to talk to, you know, man to man."

"Did he? I mean, did he talk about it?" She forced herself to breathe and remain calm.

"Verne said that Randy wanted his help with a project. You know my man; he can't ever say no to helping someone out." Trisha seemed to take her time with her memories.

"I know. He certainly did a lot to help me from time to time. I can't thank him enough," Laura agreed. "What sort of project was it?"

"He wanted to get rid of some old furniture in his garage. Verne said that it was so full of junk that Randy couldn't even park his car in it."

"What kind of furniture was there? Were there any old trunks or that sort of thing?" In her mind, Laura tried to calm her excitement and not alarm her friend about the suspicions she and Patrick shared.

"Verne brought one of the dressers home for us, but he said the rest was just trash. If I remember right, he said there was an old ratty couch and some side chairs, the kind from the early sixties. I don't think there were any old trunks. Are you looking for one?"

"I'm always looking for antiques. I need an old trunk for my guest room. It's a great place to store extra blankets and pillows." She shrugged her shoulders. "I'd better get going. Some jerk tried to break in my house last night and my handyman is there fixing it."

"You be careful, young lady. There's a lot of weirdos out there." Just as she started to shut her car door, she heard Trisha one more time.

"Oh, I just thought of this. One of those projects Verne helped him with was pouring a new back patio. Isn't that strange? With his wife missing, you'd think he would be out looking for her instead of doing home projects. Some people are just weird." Trisha didn't wait for a response but waved over her shoulder as she went back into her house.

It was all Laura could do to start her car and drive carefully and slowly back to her house. Her mind was racing with scrambled thoughts and suppositions. Before she could reach her home, her cell rang, and Laura saw it was her sister.

"Hey, Vicky. What's up?"

"Where are you?" No greeting, just emotion on the other end of the line.

"I'm heading home. Where are you?"

"I took the day off. How about meeting me at Charley's?"

Guilt surged through her body, but Laura pushed it back. "Sure, I'm close. Are you sick? Why didn't you go into work?"

"I'm fine. See you in a few." Vicky was elusive.

The turn at the next light took Laura to Charley's. She was apprehensive but wanted this chance to talk with her sister. Even though she had only done a little bit of investigation into the death of Randy's first wife, Laura felt she had enough information to convince her sister to move out and stay safe.

The parking lot was a little crowded as it was close to the lunch hour, but she managed to find a spot close to her sister's car. As she found her way into the dark space, Laura found Vicky at their usual table in the back.

Her sister waved and smiled. "Hey, sis. I ordered you a wine even though it's still early."

"Thanks. What's up?" She tried to act casually as she bent down and hugged her sister.

Once seated, Laura tried to ignore her sister's obvious anger. "Thanks for my wine."

"What in the hell do you think you're doing?" Vicky finally challenged.

"I'm not sure what you're talking about." Laura had a long drink of her wine.

"Laura, we've never lied to each other. I confided in you and now you've made my life even more miserable, if that's even possible." The tears fell from her sister's eyes.

"I would never hurt you. You have to know that." She reached across the table and took her sister's hand in hers. "Vicky, I love you and only want what's best for you."

Her sister hung her head down and openly cried. "Oh, my God, I know that. Things are so screwed up.

Randy came home and told me that you were causing trouble at the college and talking with his crew. I just assumed the worst."

"Vicky, get some clothes together and come stay with me." When she saw the protest on her sister's face, she pleaded, "Please, it doesn't have to be forever. It's just until we know you're safe."

It was more than a few minutes, but Vicky finally looked her sister in the eye. "La, I'm scared." She used her childhood name for her sister.

Laura got up and came over to sit next to her. As they hugged, she felt the tears starting to form. "Vicky, please, come and stay. If we can figure this out and Randy is not guilty, you can go back and try to save your marriage. I just want to make sure you're safe."

"Okay." Her answer was simple. "I'll go home and get some things."

"Do you want me to go with you?" Laura offered.

"No, I'll just slip in and out. I'll text when I'm on my way."

"Please, be careful."

"You're scaring me."

"I don't mean to, but Patrick and I have started to investigate, and we are very suspicious of Randy and his behavior. Please be careful."

"I better go before he comes home." They both got up and as they left Charley's, they hugged once again.

"I'll see you in a few." Vicky said.

Five

Laura wanted to follow Vicky but resisted the urge. Instead, she called Patrick. He answered on the first ring.

"Are you okay?" His response was abrupt.

"Yes, I'm fine. I'm sorry to bother you, but I've got some very interesting information."

"I'm almost done here for now, however it might take me another hour. How about I pick up some dinner and we can talk at your house."

"Better make it dinner for three." She replied.

"Oh, will Sunny be there?"

"Uh, no, my sister is coming to stay for a few days." Laura waited for his reaction.

"Wow. How did that happen? Does she know about me and what we are doing?"

"When I told her that you and I had started to investigate, she didn't seem surprised. She didn't even ask who you were, as though she already knew."

"That's interesting. Okay, I'll see you later with something for dinner. Anything in particular you'd like?" His voice was all business.

"No, you decide. Or better yet, I can make spaghetti. I have everything I need at home to do that."

"Actually, that sounds great. I'll bring the wine." With their plans settled, they hung up and Laura drove home. She checked the time on her phone before entering her kitchen. She put her purse down, noticed the bill from the handyman and went to her bedroom. Laura smiled with satisfaction when she saw the new window glass.

Keeping busy always soothed her nerves, as evidenced by the destruction of the back deck. Taking the ingredients out of the cabinet, Laura started her homemade spaghetti sauce. Normally she liked to simmer her sauce for several hours, but today it had to be a shorter version. She sliced, diced, and chopped her way through the process. Soon, the sauce was simmering on the back burner of her stove.

Checking the time on the clock in her kitchen for what seemed like the millionth time, Laura finally reached for her phone. She sent a quick text to Vicky and tried to wait patiently for her response. Going into her office, Laura grabbed her notebook and started writing notes about the conversation she'd had with Trisha. The mind can play tricks on a person and knowing that, she wanted to get it all written down before she forgot something important.

She picked up her phone, looking for a response, but found none. Her mind was starting to fill with all sorts of horrible thoughts. *Should I call Vicky?*

Should I send another text? What if Randy is there? What do I do?

Just as she decided to make the call, her phone buzzed. "On my way." Vicky finally responded.

Feeling a huge sense of relief, Laura began to prepare the guest bedroom for her sister. She grabbed clean sheets and made the bed. Taking the dirty laundry to her utility room kept her busy with her cleaning tasks. Between trips back and forth, Laura stirred the sauce simmering on the back burner. One of her trips between the bedroom and the laundry room found her reaching for the wine in the refrigerator. Pouring a small amount, she sat at the breakfast bar and waited.

A knock at the back door startled her out of her secret thoughts. Jumping up, she rushed to open the door to reveal Patrick standing there. "Oh, I'm glad you're here first."

His smile was immediate and as he stepped in, Patrick noticed the glass of wine at the bar. "I'll have some of that, if you don't mind."

She hurried to fill a glass for him as they sat together at the bar. "Vicky's on her way but I wanted to tell you about my conversation with Trisha before my sister gets here. I'm not sure how much you want Vicky to know."

"I think we need to tread carefully. She's already on alert and we don't want Randy to know what we've learned." He saw the protest forming on her lips. "Laura, they've been together for over ten years now. For better or worse, they've formed a bond, and we are on the outside. Yes, even you are just the sister."

"I understand. I don't like it, but I agree with you."

"What did Trisha tell you?" He pushed her for details.

With an excited look on her face, Laura related the details of their conversation. She referred to the notes she'd just made in her notebook. "Isn't that unusual behavior? I mean the man just lost his wife and he's cleaning out a garage and working around the house. What do you think?"

"You did good. Every bit of information we add to our growing pile of evidence helps. What sticks out in your mind?"

"I was excited about the furniture until I found there was nothing very big." She noted the knowing look on his handsome face. "Okay, nothing big enough to hold a whole body. Ewww! I can't imagine someone sick enough to chop up a human being."

"Laura, I've been trying to tell you in a way that won't completely gross you out that there are very bizarre people out there." He shook his head.

"You must have seen the worst side of humanity. I'm so sorry for that." There was a moment between them. "How do you keep it from making you crazy?"

"At first, I drank, a lot."

"Then?" Her heart was intrigued.

"I started separating myself from the evil in them. I had a wonderful wife, great kids, and a love for life. Eventually, I even became able to feel sorry for those terribly sick individuals." He took a sip of his wine, and she got up to stir the sauce. They both seemed to resist the strong emotions flowing between them.

Before they had to respond to the vibes in the room, a tentative knock came at the kitchen door, but the person behind the sound didn't wait and came on in. Vicky glanced from her sister to Patrick, her uncomfortable state showing on her face.

Laura came around and hugged her sister. "Vicky, I'd like you to meet Patrick Dickson."

Patrick got up and came over with his hand out. "I've heard such good things about you from your sister. May I help you with your bag?" He took her small duffle and headed to the guest room, giving the sisters a moment alone.

"He's good-looking." Vicky volunteered.

"Is that all you have to say?"

"Is he the detective who is helping you?" Vicky asked.

"He is retired but yes, he's agreed to help me figure out what happened to Randy's first wife. He's really a nice guy." Laura stated.

"How much does he know?" Vicky sat on the third stool at the breakfast bar.

"I know that your sister loves you a lot and we're both worried for you." Patrick's voice came across the room.

"If you have more of that wine, I'll take a glass." Vicky spoke to Laura.

"I'd like to try and put you at ease. I'm here because Laura asked me to be. I'm not here to do anything but apply logic and facts to the case. If someone is innocent, then what we uncover will prove it." Patrick sat down between the sisters.

"What did you tell Randy about coming here?" Laura asked.

"I left a note saying that we needed some space, and that I was coming here for a few days to get my head straight." She looked from side to side at Patrick and Laura. "I don't know how he's going to take it." Her nerves were showing.

"I'm here for you, Sis. You'll be fine and we'll just take it easy. You're so right about needing some space. It can't hurt." Laura reassured her.

"Well, here's to finding some peace, at least for now." Vicky raised her glass and they made a toast. "I have to be honest, especially with you, Patrick. I'm very nervous. This is a terrible situation and I'm not sure what it's all about."

Laura looked at him. Patrick immediately spoke, "Vicky, I don't mean to make you nervous. I'm just here to help your sister. We both want you to feel safe in your life and your marriage. Please relax as much as you can."

"That's a lot easier said than done, you know." Vicky responded.

Laura took her by the shoulders and gave her a little hug. "We just want to make sure you're going to be safe, and you can put all of this behind you. Why don't you two sit at the table and I'll put on the spaghetti. We'll eat as soon as it's done."

Laura then busied herself with finishing their dinner. She put together a salad and prepared the loaf of garlic bread to heat in the oven. Trying hard not to eavesdrop, Laura found her attention wandering to their conversation. Patrick and Vicky seemed to be getting along. She wanted to be a fly on the wall and listen to their conversation, but dinner preparations demanded her immediate attention.

Vicky came over after a bit to refill their drinks. "Patrick said he brought some more wine. Is that what you want for us?"

"Yes, it's over there on the counter. Get some clean glasses for the red wine and set the table. I'm almost done here."

"What can I do?" Patrick was close by.

"How about getting that garlic toast from the oven. There are some hot pads in that drawer." She pointed.

In no time at all, they were seated and sharing their meal. Laura put the food on the table, family style, and let each person help themselves. She couldn't help but notice her sister checking her phone but decided to ignore it.

"This is very good." Patrick broke the silence.

"Thank you."

"My sister makes the best homemade spaghetti sauce. I love it." Vicky agreed.

"I didn't get this one started as soon as I usually do, but I do have to admit it came out pretty good. Please help yourselves to more. I can't seem to make just a little."

Vicky nearly jumped out of her skin when her phone buzzed. She saw who was calling and stood up, "I'm going to take this outside." Before she could step out the back door, Laura shouted, "Don't go out there. The deck is gone!"

The look on her sister's face showed her exasperation. She finally went out the side door to the front of the house. Patrick looked to Laura, "That's probably Randy."

Laura laughed, "Good guess, detective. I hope he's not being the usual ass that I've know he is capable of."

"I guess we'll know soon enough. Some more wine?" Patrick rose to fill their glasses. He'd just sat back down when the side door opened, and Vicky walked in with a puzzled look on her face.

They waited for her to speak, but she seemed to be moving in slow motion with heavy thoughts in her head. Finally, Laura pressed, "Are you okay? What did he say? Did he yell at you?"

Vicky looked at her, "He was kind and seemed to be upset, but understanding."

"In other words, he wasn't his usual self." Laura observed.

The look Vicky gave her spoke volumes. "That doesn't help, Sis. This is all very upsetting and I'm so confused."

"I know and I'm sorry. What did he say?"

"He sounded very upset, but at the same time, he agreed we needed some space. He even offered to go to counseling, something he's fought since our troubles started."

Laura avoided meeting Patrick's gaze. She felt they were both thinking the same thing – Randy was playing mind games with Vicky. "That's a good idea. Why don't you set something up tomorrow?"

Vicky pushed her plate back. "I think I've lost my appetite. Do you two mind if I go and rest? I've got a lot to think about."

"Could I ask just one question?" Patrick spoke.

"Sure, I'll try to help." Vicky offered.

"What can you tell me about Randy's daughter? Do you see her often?"

This line of questioning caught Laura totally by surprise. She looked at him, waiting for further explanation. He didn't say anything more.

"I barely know the woman. When Randy and I met, it was a long time before I even knew he had a daughter. I'm guessing, but I think she went to live with relatives back east after her mother disappeared. He's always been very closed-mouth about her. Why do you ask?"

"She was thirteen when Donna disappeared. It must have been very traumatic for a teenager to go through something like that. I just wondered if you could give me an opinion about her and her state of mind."

"I really couldn't. I only met her once or twice and it wasn't for very long. Randy and his daughter don't even speak for all I know." With that she got up and took her dishes to the sink. "I'll see you in the morning, Sis. It was nice meeting you, Patrick. Sorry I couldn't be of more help."

After she left, Patrick and Laura busied themselves with clearing away the dishes and leftovers. Finally, Patrick took Laura by the shoulders and turned her to face him. "Ask me."

"Ask you what?"

"Ask me the questions that are on your mind."

"Why did you ask Vicky about the daughter? I would have thought there would be many other things you would want to know. Where did that come from?"

"Let's go sit outside." He started to the side door.

"Want some more wine? I think I'm going to need some reinforcements." She filled their glasses and followed Patrick to the front porch.

"I love this time of year. It can be so relaxing." He sat down on one of the lawn chairs. She took the one next to him and handed him the glass of wine. "Dinner was delicious, thank you. Vicky is right, your sauce is the best."

"Thanks. I can put some in a jar to send home with you. All you have to do is make some pasta and you've got a meal."

"I'd like that."

"Now, tell me why you asked about the daughter." She pushed him.

"That's one area of this entire case that I regret most. I never got to talk with her, and I feel that she had a lot more information about her mother's disappearance than what was in the notes."

"I can't imagine a mother going off and leaving her daughter behind. As angry as I got with my son at times, I would never have left him." She sipped her glass. "This is good. I normally don't like red wine, but this is very smooth, no bite to it."

"It's one of my favorites." Patrick agreed.

"Of all the things you want to know about Randy, I would have thought you would ask Vicky about his recent behavior and the disappearance of his first wife."

"Ah, great catch. It's an interrogation technique I use to keep suspects off their game. They expect me to go right to the heart of things and when I skirt the issue, it makes them relax a bit."

"I can see how that might work. I'm sure Vicky thought you would ask something specific about Randy and why she thinks he killed his first wife." Laura looked at him at this point. "When you say 'suspect' you don't mean my sister, do you?"

"Absolutely not. She came along many years later. Unfortunately, she's gotten herself in the wrong place at the wrong time. He's a smooth one and I feel very bad for her."

"Me too. I hope I can keep her here with me for a while. It might keep her safe." Laura spoke softly and her fears showed in the tone of her voice.

"Oh, I just remembered. Another thing Trisha told me was that Verne was helping Randy put in a new patio at the back of the house."

With that, Patrick nearly choked on the sip of wine he was taking. "Why didn't you tell me that earlier? That's huge!"

As the value of this information registered in Laura's mind, she turned to face him. "Oh, my God! He buried her under the patio! Oh, how stupid can I be?"

"Laura, you're not stupid. You are one of the smartest women I know."

"How could I not catch that? Patrick, do you really believe he buried her in their own backyard?" She put her hand on his arm. "How can that be? Is he really that evil?"

"First off, let's look at the facts. We don't know that any of this is true. Our investigation must be based on truth, not supposition. That's what we're doing here. The information from Trisha needs to be checked before we jump to conclusions. Conclusion jumping can be dangerous to your health." He tried to make a joke as he put his hand on hers.

With a deep breath, Laura managed a small smile. "I guess I have a lot to learn, don't I?"

"You'll do fine." He broke their contact and stood up. "I should be going. You two will be okay?"

She followed him back to the kitchen. "Yes, I'll lock all the doors and make sure the windows are secured."

"Do you own a gun? Do you know how to handle a weapon?"

"I have my 'baby' but I'm not sure if I have any bullets."

He rolled his eyes. By this time, they were in the kitchen and Laura was filling a jar with her spaghetti sauce. "What are you doing tomorrow morning?"

"I hadn't planned anything. Why?"

"I think we need to go to the firing range. I would like you to bring your gun and meet me there."

"I don't know if Vicky will be going to work. Call me in the morning and I'll let you know."

"Be safe tonight. Keep your phone with you and call me if anything happens." He hesitated, but then left before saying anything more.

After locking the doors and checking the windows, Laura was finally satisfied that the house was secure for the night. As she went down the hall, she stopped and listened at the guest room door. The silence convinced her that her sister was asleep, and she went to her own room. Shutting the door, she finally allowed herself to relax. Once in her nightgown, Laura turned her television on low volume and crawled into bed.

The next morning and groggy from a restless night, she headed to the kitchen ready to start the coffee. The note next to the almost full pot caught her attention.

It read, "La, I'm going to work. I find it's best to keep my mind busy, given everything that's going on in my life. Thanks so much for putting up with me. See you tonight."

Filling her coffee cup, Laura texted Patrick. "I'm free to go to the firing range. Give me the address and at least an hour." She sat at the breakfast bar trying to wake up. A slow grin crossed her face as she thought about the surprise on Patrick's face when they meet at the shooting range.

Once dressed, she checked her phone and saw his reply.

His message changed their plans. "Will be over to pick you up. Bring some snacks and a drink for yourself. We might be gone a while."

Laura wasn't sure what to take but grabbed several different munchies and put everything in a small cooler along with a bottle of water and a soda. She was just adding ice to the cooler when Patrick knocked on the side door. Taking her purse and the cooler, Laura opened the door and stepped outside.

"What's up? Where are we going?" They walked side by side to the driveway. As she noticed the small car, she commented, "Where's your truck?"

"Let me ask you some questions." He opened the passenger door for her. As he squeezed in the driver's side, Patrick posed his first question. "What did you think when Vicky told you about Randy's reaction when he came home and found her gone?"

Laura opened her mouth to answer but closed it again before replying. "I'm sure you remember my initial reaction. I didn't believe it."

"Yes, that stuck in my mind, and I think Vicky was stunned that he was being so subdued and cooperative about their situation."

"So, you think he's up to something." She added, "We're going to go and spy on the lovely Randy. That explains this small nondescript car."

"Very good. You'll make a fine detective when you grow up." He teased.

She didn't respond but felt her cheeks warm a bit with his compliment. He was heading in the direction of Vicky's home but turned on a road just before they got there. These beautiful homes were built on the steep hills in Prescott and although the main road looped throughout the subdivision, there were many short streets that led to more homesites and lots. All of the homes were custom-built structures, each elegant in its own way. The curvy streets and the steep hillsides allowed for privacy and beautiful views of the city below.

"I found the perfect spot for watching their home. A general contractor started building a house on the hill just above Vicky and Randy's home, but for whatever reason it was never finished. We'll be there all by ourselves and can see directly down to their lot." Patrick carefully maneuvered the small compact into an empty dirt driveway. The partially-built house stood before them as a testament to someone's dream.

Patrick got out of the car and stretched his body. "I'm not used to such a small space. I already miss my truck."

She laughed but joined him beside the car. "Where do we want to be?"

"Come, I'll show you." To her surprise he took Laura's hand and led her around the side of the unfinished building to a small, concrete slab that had been poured at the back of the lot. Laura walked carefully to the edge and looked down at the steep terrain. "Wow, this is an amazing view. I think I'd like to finish this house and live here." Her voice showed that she was in a teasing mood. "Well, what do we do now?"

His chuckle caught her off guard. "This is the most boring part of any stakeout. We set up, then wait and wait and wait."

"I have a feeling you're not kidding me now." She faced him.

"Unfortunately, I'm not. I brought some lawn chairs. Let's unload the car and set up over there. We have some cover but still a direct view to the house." He pointed to the area.

They got the cooler and lawn chairs from the car and working together, they had their observation site set up in no time at all. Laura plopped down in her chair and sighed.

"Don't get bored yet. We have a long day ahead of us." Patrick warned.

As they sat on their lawn chairs in the middle of the day on the side of a steep hill in Prescott, Arizona, Laura wondered if she'd lost her mind. She felt a tap on her arm and was surprised to see the pair of binoculars that Patrick was handing her. "Use these and tell me what you see."

She adjusted her view until she could clearly see the house below belonging to Randy and Vicky. Moving slowly from left to right, Laura found herself pondering how different her sister's house looked from this angle. She could see the pool area and the guest room as well as the private patio outside the master bedroom.

As she took the binoculars from her eyes, Laura noticed that Patrick was using another pair to study the same area she'd just viewed. "What do you see?" She asked.

"I see a wonderful, rich space that those two people can't afford." He lowered his field glasses to look her directly in the eye, waiting for her reaction.

"You've said that before. What do you base your opinion on?" she challenged.

He thought for just a moment but answered with confidence. "How much do you think a house in this subdivision costs?"

She looked around at the lot and the unfinished house where they were sitting. "I'm betting the places in this neighborhood cost a minimum of six or seven hundred thousand."

"What does your sister make in a year? What do you think Randy is earning?"

"Okay, I get it. They're living beyond their means, but in this day and age, who doesn't?"

"I'll give you that. I just want you to think about the entire aspect of the case. Think of how they support this kind of existence. Maybe it would be easier if you thought of how Randy can afford this lifestyle."

Laura was lost in her own thoughts for a few minutes. "I have to admit my sister is not very involved in their finances. She likes being able to buy what she wants when she wants it. She's always been a bit elusive about their spending."

"I know this is not easy for you. I appreciate that you're trying to look at the entire situation with an open mind." He turned back to look through his binoculars at the view below.

"I have a question for you." She finally voiced out loud.

As Patrick kept staring, he said, "Ask away."

"What in the world do you do with yourself on these stakeouts?" Her laughter was addictive, and Patrick joined in with her joke.

Patrick responded with a compliment she didn't expect. "At least I have someone nice to talk to this time and we have a wonderful view." "You should see some of the sleazy places I've been holed up in while watching a suspect."

"I can only imagine. I have watched enough old detective shows to put some sordid pictures in my mind."

"The sitcoms were the best. They always put a funny twist on what should be a very serious situation. I really enjoy those shows."

Laura took this opportunity to tell him something that had been on her mind. "Umm, I feel the need to let you know a little about my past."

That got his attention. "Are you a wanted criminal on the lam?" He started to laugh but when he saw the look on her face, he stopped. "Seriously, Laura, you couldn't possibly have something that bad in your background."

She squirmed in her lawn chair before answering. "It was a long time ago, in fact, Carl and I had only been married about five years. An old girlfriend of his started stalking us. She came to the house and rammed my car, threw eggs on the house and ran over the mailbox. She even came to a local bar that we all went to after work. She started telling everyone about my personal stuff, most of it was lies."

"Did you file a police report?" His official demeanor kicked in as he listened to her tale.

"Yes, we did report it the night she hit my car. She even came back and hit it again. The police searched but didn't find her that night. I thought that would be it and she'd give up and leave us alone."

"But she didn't." He stated the obvious.

"No, she kept trying to get into our workplace, but security turned her away. So, she continued to go to the bar and spread the same rumors. It finally came to a boil one night at the bar. She was there and I saw her go into the bathroom. Carl wasn't there so I had my friend come with me and once in there, my friend watched the door, while I beat the crap out of that crazy woman!"

He couldn't help but laugh. "I'm sorry, but I just can't see you doing something like that."

"I'm not proud of it, but she had pushed and pushed until I felt myself snap. We left her lying there on the floor in the bathroom. I went back to the table, finished my drink and went home. Carl was home, and I told him that we needed to go to see the police."

"What happened then? Were charges filed against you?"

"No, not then, but she later filed a police report." She waited for his reaction.

"What happened after that?"

"It was supposed to go to court. We had filed charges against her for the damage to my car and the house, so it was a mess. I went to the bar the next day and apologized to the owner. We knew him and I wanted to know if I would be kicked out for causing trouble. He told me the police had been there investigating the incident."

"You must have been scared." Patrick commented.

"I was scared, ashamed and just wanted the whole thing to go away. It finally did. We both just dropped the charges and nothing ever came of it."

Laura finally looked his way and started laughing. "I can't believe I felt the need to tell you my deep dark secret and it happened such a long time ago."

He joined in her laughter. "I still can't picture you beating someone."

Through giggles, Laura confessed, "When I first grabbed her by the hair and flung her to the floor, my thoughts were 'wow, she's so light.' At the end, I had her on the floor. I stood over her and told her if she didn't stop stalking me, I'd kill her." She completed her thoughts, "I just wanted you to know that I have a mean streak in me when pushed too far."

Suddenly Patrick was alert. She followed his gaze and saw why. A small rental truck was pulling in the drive of her sister's home below. The truck went past the house and slowly pulled up next to a small outbuilding. Patrick and Laura looked through their binoculars and watched Randy get out of the truck. He unlocked the big garage door and looked around before entering the building.

"You were right! He is up to something alright!" She stared as Randy carried box after box out of the garage, loading them in the back of the truck. "We need to get into that truck and see what's in those boxes." She lowered the binoculars to look directly at Patrick and noticed he was taking pictures with his cell phone. He stopped at her words.

"You're absolutely right!"

Six

"I'm sorry. I don't think I heard you correctly. Did you just admit that I was right?" Laura challenged.

Her words were interrupted by movement below. Laura and Patrick both quickly trained their view on the action. Randy continued bringing boxes out of the storage space, but soon he pulled the door down on the back of the truck. "He's finished." She stated. "What now?"

"We have to follow him and see where he's taking those boxes." Patrick stood up but hesitated.

"He might see me and that won't be good. You go and I'll wait here for you." She volunteered. "Patrick, he's getting back into the truck. You need to hurry."

"I can't leave you here alone."

"I'll call Sunny. She can come and get me. Go! We can't miss out on finding what he's doing with all the boxes." She pushed at him. "I'll be fine. Keep texting me and let me know what's going on."

"Don't do anything but wait here. Let me know when Sunny gets here." He got into the small rental car and sped away.

Laura quickly sent a text to her granddaughter. While she waited for a response, she watched as the rental truck pulled out onto the street below and saw that Patrick was slowly driving down the same road, not too far behind Randy.

Seeing the text from Sunny, Laura was dismayed that her granddaughter couldn't come to get her for at least an hour. What am I going to do? Her mind rambled with thoughts of Patrick and Randy. She looked over the edge of the hillside and realized that although the terrain was rough, it wasn't impassable. A plan was forming in her mind. Without further hesitation, Laura started down the side of the hill towards her sister's house below.

It wasn't easy. Laura considered herself reasonably fit and kept trekking toward her destination. Vicky had given her a set of keys to the house and with that she hoped she could get into that room. Maybe there were still boxes in storage and she could get some pictures of what Randy was hiding.

Laura got a text from Patrick stating he was still in pursuit. He wanted to make sure that Sunny was on her way to pick her up. With fast fingers, she told him that all was okay, and she'd be home soon. It wasn't an exact lie, just a 'delayed' timeline. Laura felt confident that all would be well when they connected later, and her little white lie wouldn't hurt.

After slipping several times down the steep embankment, Laura finally found herself walking up to the storage room. She pulled out her key ring and tried several keys but none of them opened the padlock. Walking around the building she found a side door, but it too was locked tight. The building had no windows and Laura soon realized that her attempts to discover any clues were fruitless.

Her phone buzzed and she saw that Patrick was giving his update. He stated that Randy had finally pulled into a storage unit all the way down in Mayer, a small, rural town about thirty minutes away. The small-town atmosphere didn't allow him to get too close, but he had managed to park a few blocks away without being discovered by their suspect. He walked towards the building, trying to be as inconspicuous as possible.

Laura answered back but didn't elaborate. About the same time, Sunny said she was on her way. Laura quickly texted her granddaughter to pick her up at Vicky's house, ending with the word 'Hurry'.

Finally deciding to enter the house, Laura went into the kitchen. Trying not to touch anything, she sat at the breakfast bar. Curiosity got the best of her, and she found herself wandering into the office area. The house was not as clean as her sister would have kept it, but her sister's life was in upheaval right now. A sudden thought occurred, maybe he kept an extra set of keys in his desk.

She was slowly opening the lap drawer of the big oak desk and found exactly what she was looking for when she heard a squeaky female voice behind her. "Nana, what are you doing?"

She jumped back and screamed. "Sunny! You scared the hell out of me!"

"Why are you here? Where is your car?"

"Let's get out of here." Just then her phone chimed. As she looked at the screen, her heart was in for another shock. Patrick texted, "He's on his way back. I'll meet you at your house."

"We've got to get out of here. Randy's on his way back and he can't see me here." She grabbed the key ring from the drawer and pushed her granddaughter towards the back door.

"Too late." Sunny pointed out the side window. "He's here." They both saw the small rental truck pulling into the driveway next to the storage room.

Faster than she thought she could move, Laura went to the door of the garage. "Don't let him know I'm here." She shut the door after ducking into the darkened garage.

Sunny watched her uncle looking over her car before coming into the kitchen. She was sitting on the barstool, sipping a soda. "Hey, Uncle, what's up?"

His casual attitude was forced, but Randy appeared to accept his niece sitting in his kitchen. "What're you doing here? Vicky isn't home."

"I know. She promised I could borrow her little glitter purse. I'm getting ready for prom, and I want to match the color of my dress."

"Did you find the purse?" He helped himself to a beer from the fridge.

"No, I didn't look for it yet. I just got here and was thirsty. Are you off work already?" She posed an innocent question.

"No, I have to get back to the college." She saw him head to the garage door and quickly jumped up from the stool. "Wait!"

He stopped at her command. "What? You know where Vicky keeps her stuff. Go and get it." He moved forward with his hand on the doorknob to the garage.

"Uncle Randy, I know that you and Vicky are split up and I feel kinda funny going through her things without you seeing what I take. Please, come with me. I promise I'll be quick, and you can get back to work."

With a disgusted grunt, Randy gave in and waved his hand to indicate she should go ahead to the back of the house. "Hurry, I've been gone too long, and they might miss me at work." His sarcasm was obvious as he walked down the hallway behind Sunny.

She went to the closet and found a shelf with her aunt's purses. Rifling through them slowly, she hoped she'd give her Nana enough time to get out of the garage and out of the house.

"Come on! I'm in a hurry." Randy insisted.

"Here it is! Isn't this pretty?" With shaking hands, Sunny grinned. "Thank you, Uncle. I'll get out of your hair now." She bounded out the door and down the hallway but realized he was close behind.

"Thanks!" She waved the purse above her head and as quick as she could, went out the back door and got into her car.

"Nana? Are you here?" She spoke quietly while putting on her seatbelt.

"Yes, just drive!" An anxious voice came from the floor of the backseat.

Sunny raised her hand to wave at Randy, who was standing on the back patio. She gave him a grin and pulled onto the roadway. Once she got to the small shopping center at the end of Lee Boulevard, Sunny pulled into a parking space and allowed her grandmother to get in the front seat.

"Go! What are you waiting for?" Laura asked with panic in her voice.

"Nana, don't you think it's about time that you fill me in on what you're doing?"

With a big sigh, she put her hand on Sunny's shoulder. "Let's get to my house. Patrick is waiting and I'm sure he's not going to be at all happy with me. We'll talk together."

Before putting her car into gear, Sunny looked at her favorite person in the entire world. "Nana, you have my word. I can keep a secret."

"Okay, sweetie, let's just go. My nerves are stretched to the max. I want to thank you for stopping your uncle from coming into the garage. I thought I would be discovered for sure."

Soon they were on the road. As they pulled up to her house, they saw Patrick standing by his car with a look of disgust on his handsome face, his arms crossed over his chest. "Be prepared, little one. He's not happy."

Patrick waited for them to park, not moving, nor changing his expression. Taking a step and straightening her back, Laura walked over and faced him. She decided the direct approach would be the best. "I saw an opportunity and I took it, just like you did."

"Hi, Patrick." Sunny joined the tense situation. "I got Nana home safe."

"Thank you for that, although she wasn't in harm's way when I left her."

"Can we go in the house? Let's have something to eat and drink. You can fill me in on what you found out." Laura proposed.

Reluctantly, Patrick finally undid his hands and taking Sunny's extended hand, he followed Laura to the side door and into the kitchen. Laura went to the refrigerator and pulled out the sandwich makings she'd bought earlier, setting things on the table as fast as she could. "Sunny, get us some drinks...and no, you can't have wine."

"Patrick, what would you like? I know Nana wants some wine."

They kept busy gathering the ingredients for their impromptu meal. Laura tried to ignore Patrick's mood and hoped they could settle their differences before the night was over. Sunny put a cold bottle of beer in front of him. As they all finally sat down, facing each other, Laura spoke, "I know you're not happy, but we are all sitting here, safe and sound."

"Laura, I've tried to tell you, this is not a game. It is life and death we are dealing with, and I'll not have any part in putting you or your granddaughter in harm's way."

"Let's just eat and then we can talk." Laura started building her own sandwich, ignoring the major tension in the room.

Patrick agreed, "Thank you, I am hungry." He reached for the sandwich makings. Soon they were all eating and the mood in the room seemed to ease a bit. Laura started clearing the remnants of their meal when Sunny spoke directly to Patrick. "I know that you and my Nana are working on Aunt Vicky's case. I've told her that I can be trusted to keep a secret. So, I'm hoping that you two will share what's going on and how I can help."

Leave it to a youngster to get right to the point, Laura thought as she listened to Sunny. Patrick looked to Laura, "Please sit down so we can talk." His tone was more subdued, and she instantly felt that he was calming down.

Getting Patrick another beer and filling her wine, Laura sat back down at the table. She waited for him to talk. It didn't take long.

"What do you want to do?" He posed the question to Laura. "How much do you want to tell Sunny?"

"I think she should know everything as long as she totally understands how serious this is and we set parameters."

"I've already told you that I can keep a secret and I will." Sunny confirmed her oath.

"I will emphasize this again, I want you both to understand that this is serious business." He turned to Sunny. "I was one of the investigators in the disappearance of your uncle's first wife. I think he killed her but couldn't prove it." He looked at Laura.

Laura spoke as she reached over to pat her granddaughter's hand, "Sunny, you need to agree to keep all of this to yourself. You can't talk to anyone, not your dad, your friends, and especially not even your Aunt Vicky."

"This is not a game, Sunny. I've seen more human drama than you or your grandmother can imagine. When cornered, a killer will do whatever they have to do to survive. People can be evil. Neither of you can imagine the gruesome cases I've had to work on."

"Do you really think that he killed his first wife?" Sunny's small voice was the only sound in the kitchen.

"We don't know for sure, but everything I've learned so far tells me that it's a distinct possibility. Please, Sunshine, I don't want you involved if you have any doubts. I want you safe and sound." Laura pleaded.

Sunny hesitated but just for a second. "Nana, I never really liked Uncle Randy. When he looks at me, it's creepy. I want to help if I can."

"Then we're all on the same page." Patrick confirmed.

"Yes, I understand that this is all between just the three of us. No one else can know." Sunny agreed and the three of them clasped hands together. It was a moment Laura hoped she wouldn't regret.

"So, what's the plan?" Sunny asked in an exuberant voice.

"What did you find out?" Laura pointed her question to Patrick.

"Randy took the boxes to a local storage unit down in Mayer. I found out the number of the unit but other than that, the trip wasn't very useful."

"I tried to get into that storage room behind their house but none of the keys that Vicky has given me fit the lock." Laura relayed.

"What were you doing in the office when I came to get you?" Sunny asked.

Laura looked at Patrick before giving her answer. "I thought maybe I would find the extra set of keys for that room."

"That brings us to an agreement I need from both of you." Patrick interrupted. "I kept you informed the entire time I was tailing Randy. I expect the same from both of you. It's the only way we're going to stay safe."

"You're right. I should've told you what I was doing." Laura admitted.

"I sure would have liked to know what was going on when you texted me to come and get you, Nana." Sunny interjected. "You know how easily I can get distracted. You could have been caught."

"Then, we're all agreed. We'll keep information flowing between us all." Patrick reached out and placed his hand palm up on the table. Each one placed their hand on top as a show of cooperation.

"We need one last commitment." Patrick looked each of them in the eye before continuing, "No one but the three of us can learn about what we are doing."

"I agree." Laura said.

"I, too, agree." Sunny gave her word.

"Did you find extra keys?" he asked Laura.

She reached into her pocket and pulled out a big ring of miscellaneous keys. "I know now I shouldn't have taken them, but I was startled by Sunny and just grabbed them. We'll have to get them back in the desk somehow."

Patrick reached over and held the ring of keys in his hand. One by one, he inspected the keys. He finally held up two. "These might be to a padlock. I'll get these duplicated and then we'll figure out how to get them back in the desk without Randy knowing they were missing. Where exactly were those keys?"

"Maybe I can do it." Sunny volunteered.

"No!" A definite no came from both Patrick and Laura simultaneously.

"Whoa! Whoa! I get it." Sunny held up her hands.

"We won't involve you in anything that could endanger you in any way." Laura spoke firmly to her. Then to Patrick, she explained the exact placement of the keys in the drawer of the desk.

"How can I help then?" The young woman wanted so badly to be of use to the investigation.

"Right now, just keep your promise and we'll let you know when we need some extra help." Patrick tried to pacify her natural exuberance.

"I understand. You two just need to let me know."

Interrupting their conversation, the side door opened, and Vicky stepped in to greet them. "Sunny! I'm glad you're here." As a second thought, she turned to Laura and Patrick. "Hey, how are you two?"

"I'm good. Want something to eat? We still have plenty." Laura offered, trying to contain her nerves.

"No, thanks. I had a big lunch. I got off work early today." Vicky put her purse down and came to sit at the table. "Sunny, I got a call from Randy. He said you were at the house today. Why?"

"You said I could borrow a purse for my prom. Remember? We talked about it a few weeks ago." She got up and retrieved the handbag to show her aunt.

"Oh, my, I do vaguely remember that conversation, but why did you go today? Surely, you must know that Randy and I have temporarily separated?" She looked to her sister for an explanation.

"I did tell her." Laura confirmed.

"That's why I went when I thought he'd be at work. I feel weird about this whole situation, and I didn't want to run into him, but I did anyway. Is that a problem?" Sunny asked innocently.

"Oh, man. This is so hard." Vicky shook her head. "I never thought I would be in a spot like this. I just wanted to be married and live happily ever after."

"Do you want something to drink?" Patrick stood up.

"Yes, I do. I'll take some of that wine."

Much to Laura's surprise at Patrick acting the host, she waited for her sister to calm down a bit. He set the glass in front of her. "Randy was upset, then?"

"Yes, he chewed on me for at least fifteen minutes. I don't appreciate being caught off guard like that."

"I can understand that." Patrick empathized. "Didn't you wonder what he was doing home at that time?"

"As a matter of fact, I didn't at the time, but as I drove here, it definitely crossed my mind." She took a long sip of her drink. "Mom always taught us that you have to play the cards you're dealt, but I never wanted a losing hand like this!"

Laura got up and hugged her sister. Tears were forming in Vicky's eyes as she looked around the table. "I've got to ask you to give me the house keys back, Sunny. I don't want to aggravate him any more than I have to."

"Auntie, I'm so sorry. I didn't mean to cause you any trouble. I just wanted to pick up the purse." Sunny tried to explain. "I made him go with me to your closet so that he could see I wasn't taking anything else."

"Oh, I know you wouldn't do any harm. It's just that I'm not sure where this is going to end up and I'm not ready to be divorced." Vicky responded. There was a lot of thinking going around that table, but finally, Vicky turned to her niece. "Did your uncle say anything about why he was at the house? He has a lot of freedom at the college, he can come and go without too much effort. I just don't remember him coming home in the middle of the afternoon."

"He didn't say anything. He got a beer from the fridge but just waited for me to find this purse."

"He drank a beer? In the middle of the day? That doesn't make any sense."

"I'm sure his world is as upset as yours." Patrick offered an explanation.

"Randy's been at the college for over twenty years. He wouldn't jeopardize his retirement for anything. Lately, it's as if I don't know that man! I've been married to him for almost ten years. He's gone all the time; he doesn't talk to me, and we never do anything together anymore." She got up and helped herself to more wine.

Looks passed between Patrick and Laura. Sunny sat silently, observing the tactics he seemed to be using to get information from Vicky. She got up and picked up her purse. Retrieving the key ring, she started to remove the house key for her aunt.

"I'm so sorry, Patrick. You must think I'm a total nutcase." As she sat back down at the table, Vicky waited for him to speak.

In a quiet, controlled voice, Patrick spoke, "I don't think you're a nut. I feel like you're a woman in pain and drowning in conflict and confusion."

Her tears started to flow more freely as Laura tried to contain her emotions. This man, Laura thought, this man is something else. His calming voice broke into her thoughts, "Vicky, I think the best thing you're doing right now is taking time away from Randy."

Sunny handed the single key to her aunt. "I'm so sorry."

Vicky reached up and took the key from her. She stood up and hugged her niece tightly, noting the sadness on her young face. "Oh, sweetie, you did nothing wrong. This is not your fault and certainly not your mess." Sunny gave her a soft kiss on the cheek. "Just be happy, Auntie."

"Nana, Patrick, I'm going home. I'll talk with you tomorrow." The look she gave them confirmed her promise to keep things quiet.

With the hustle and bustle of Sunny leaving, Vicky drank another glass of wine, Patrick observed, and Laura kissed her granddaughter at the back door. "Text me when you get home."

"I need to get this key back to Randy." She gave her sister a sad look. "I should probably get yours back too. He's always been such a control freak and with us split up, I think he doesn't want my family cleaning him out."

"That's absurd! We wouldn't do anything like that." Laura protested.

"I think it's a very normal reaction, especially from a man." Patrick spoke up. His look at Laura added unsaid words. She understood.

"I have no idea what's normal at this point. If you get your key, I'll take them to the house."

"I don't think that's a good idea right now. You've had several drinks and if you wait a little bit, I can go with you." Laura offered.

"You're probably right. I think I'll go and take a quick nap. I'm so exhausted." She stumbled a bit but got up and headed to the guest room. They heard the bedroom door shut.

"I'll duplicate those keys and retrieve our chairs from the lookout point. Keep her here." He was out the door before Laura could offer any objections.

She kept herself busy clearing away their meal offerings. Several times she went to the guest bedroom door to listen, but with no sound coming from the room, she was convinced her sister had fallen asleep.

I don't know if I'm cut out to be an investigator, she thought to herself. Her nerves were stretched to the limit, and she felt the second hand on her kitchen clock had slowed down to a crawl. How were they going to get those keys back in the house without Randy knowing?

Going to her office and logging onto her computer, Laura looked at the pictures of the questions she had originally painted on the wall. As she studied them, one question stood out. Where was Randy's daughter? What had she seen the night her mother disappeared? With determination, Laura started to randomly search. She first searched for Randy Bell. She worked to see what, if anything, she could find out about the first wife, the daughter, or any sort of information that would help them.

"What are you doing?" Patrick's voice made her jump.

"You scared me! I didn't hear you come in." She whirled around in her chair to see him leaning in the doorway. "You people have got to stop doing that!"

He held his hands up with a mocking look on his face. "You people? Who else has scared you?"

"I guess it's my fault. I get so involved in whatever project I'm working on that I completely zone out."

"You do need to work on your observation skills if you're going to be a successful investigator. Come on out to the kitchen."

"Did you get the keys duplicated?" She was curious.

"Yes, and I successfully put the ring of keys back into his desk."

She was surprised. "You went into their house? Where was Randy?"

"When I went to get the chairs, I noticed that the truck wasn't there, so I took the opportunity to check out some things by myself."

"Wait a minute! Didn't we all just sit here and agree that no one would make a move without letting the others know?" Laura challenged him.

Patrick held up his hand in surrender. "You're absolutely right and I was wrong to make you agree to that. I think in all honesty, it's just my inability to trust your instincts. Laura, we've just met a few days ago and we hardly know each other."

"That's true. You and I don't know each other, but we'll learn as we go along. I think you can see that I'm a responsible adult with a good sense of right and wrong. I won't do anything that puts me in danger. I may take a few chances now and then, but it's in the search for the truth."

"Okay, we'll both give the other the benefit of the doubt. Now, do you want to know what I found?" His brown eyes lit up.

Laura put her fingers to her lips to silence him before sneaking into the hallway. When she returned just seconds later, she told him, "I wanted to make sure Vicky wasn't awake. I think she's starting to lose it. This is hard enough without knowing all the details that we've learned."

"You're such a good sister. I agree with you about keeping this information from her until we have definite proof. With what I saw in that small building out back, I'd say our boy Randy is in the business of breaking and entering. That garage is full of stuff."

"What was in there?" Her curiosity was piqued.

"There are television sets, stereos, paintings, tools, and boxes full of jewelry, silverware, and computers. I didn't get to look through everything, but he must have thousands of dollars worth of goods."

"That's how he can afford to live in that beautiful custom house. He must be breaking into homes and stealing everything you saw. That must be why he's gone all the time." She thought for a moment and added, "He couldn't possibly do this all by himself, could he?"

"I'm sure he can't. We need to find out who else is involved. This investigation is growing, and the more people involved, the more danger we could be in as we get closer to solving this mystery." His cell chimed and Patrick quickly answered as soon as he saw the name on the screen.

Laura listened to Patrick's end of the conversation and immediately knew it pertained to their investigation. As soon as he got off the phone, he relayed the details. "My guy found Randy's daughter, Lisa. She's willing to talk with us!"

Seven

"Patrick, that's great! When can we meet with her?" Laura had to contain herself from jumping up and giving the man a big hug.

"Well, it won't be a face-to-face meeting, but she said she would talk with us on the internet."

"Darn, I'd love to see her actual reactions. The internet seems to dilute one's personality." Laura commented.

"I agree, but at least this will be better than nothing. Let's list the questions we'd like to ask. Do you have a tablet?"

"Of course, I'll get it." Laura got up and grabbed a pad from the desk in the office and returned to the kitchen table.

For the next half-hour or so, she and Patrick worked on the questions they'd like to ask Randy's daughter. After looking at their list, Laura said, "I doubt we'll get half of these questions answered, but at least we can try."

"The most important thing you'll find in interrogation techniques is that whatever we ask, they'll provide clues without realizing they did."

"Oh, I get it. We ask one thing and as they try to avoid giving information, they indirectly give us clues that might be valuable." She looked at the list again.

"You got it! Good job!" He complimented her.

They were interrupted by Vicky's voice. "What are you two up to now?"

"Hey, sis, there's coffee over there. You want some?" As she spoke, Laura turned the notepad over to hide their notes.

As her sister filled a coffee cup, Laura and Patrick exchanged knowing glances. "Did you have a good nap?"

"I've heard that depressed people sleep more. Do you think that's true?" Vicky sat at the table.

"Sweetie, I think you're going to be fine. Don't try to analyze it all, just try to take care of yourself." Laura reached over and patted her sister's hand.

"Are you ready to give Randy the keys? I feel that I need to do that much." Vicky looked at Laura.

Without looking at Patrick, Laura agreed. "Sure, I'm ready when you are. I'll drive."

Patrick stood up. "I'm heading home. I have work to do for a client. See you later." As he headed to the side door, Laura spoke, "I'll call you when I get ready for your help on my back deck." She hoped he'd get her subliminal message.

"That's great. Have you ordered the materials?"

"Yes. The order should be delivered here in the next day or so." Laura answered.

"Thanks, Patrick, for putting up with me." Vicky's embarrassment was obvious.

"Trust me, I just want what's best for you. It isn't a problem." His answer reinforced the feelings Laura was starting to have for the new man in her life.

After he left, the two sisters looked at each other. "La, I'm so sorry I've become a burden." Vicky fought back the tears starting to fall down her cheeks.

Grabbing her tightly, Laura tried to console her sister, "Shush, that's what sisters are for. Let's go and give those keys back to Randy. Then we can get some dinner and you can relax for a bit."

"I'd like that." Vicky agreed and together they drove to the big house on Lee Boulevard. There was little conversation on the way, but Laura could sense the nervous state her sister was in as they neared her house. As they pulled in the drive, she let out her breath. Neither his car nor the rental truck were visible, which she hoped meant he wasn't home, which her sister's words instantly confirmed.

"Well, as usual he's not home. Let's get this over with. I'll run in and put the keys on the kitchen counter. You wait here and I'll be right back." Vicky said.

"You are keeping your keys to the house, right?" Laura asked.

"Absolutely, this place is half mine, no matter what happens." She leaned in the window. "Sis, I'm not entirely dumb."

"I never said that. You're in a mixed-up state and I just wanted to remind you that you have rights. You need to take care of yourself."

"I know, I'm sorry. That's so true." She turned to the back door. "I'll be back shortly."

Laura sat there in the car, nervously looking around. She didn't want to run into Randy. Just as the thought crossed her mind, the man appeared. He drove past her car and parked close to the small outbuilding. Laura looked towards the door, hoping Vicky would appear.

His approach wasn't friendly at all. "What are you doing here?" Before she could answer his question, Vicky came out the back door and stopped dead in her tracks.

"Randy, what are you doing here?" Vicky asked as she got closer to her sister's car.

"I live here. The real question is what are you doing here? I thought we agreed to a separation." His manner was confrontational, at the very least.

"I have a right to be here. In fact, I was returning the extra keys you wanted back." They were finally face-to-face beside the car. The entire situation seemed volatile, and Laura wished she could disappear. "Vicky, just get in the car."

"Yes, Vicky, listen to your sister and get the hell out of here."

"I thought we were going to try and work out our problems. I can't believe you're being so obnoxious." She spoke bravely but moved backwards to the passenger side of the car. "I have a right to come into my own home. I will be back to get some more clothes."

With a deep breath, Randy's attitude seemed to deflate. "You should just call or text first. That way I'm not caught by surprise."

"Okay, I can do that. Maybe we can meet somewhere and have dinner." Vicky put on a weak smile.

"Sure. We need to talk some things out. I'll text you later and set it up." He was done, and headed to the door, never looking back as Laura and Vicky left.

Laura expected the waterworks and didn't have to wait long for Vicky to start crying. "I can't believe our marriage has come to this. If only he'd tell me why he's gone so much. We had so much fun when we were dating." Between sobs, she continued, "We couldn't stand to be away from each other. What in the world went wrong?"

Feeling the best reply would be no reply, Laura allowed her sister to cry. Reflecting on her own divorce, Laura was suddenly grateful that she and Carl worked hard to keep it civil. I'll have to tell him that, she thought, but immediately corrected herself. No, he doesn't need to hear from me. Best to leave sleeping dogs lie.

As they pulled into the driveway at Laura's, Vicky spoke. She'd calmed down for the moment. "La, I'm just going to go to my bedroom. I feel I need to be alone."

"Do what you want. I know it must be hard on you. I'll call you for dinner."

Once in the kitchen, Laura poured some of the cold coffee and heated it in the microwave. As she sipped the freshly-heated brew, Laura thought about the even bigger disaster her sister would be facing if they proved Randy killed his first wife. Her thoughts were interrupted by the loud noise of a big vehicle pulling up in front of her house. Looking out the window, she was thrilled to see the lumber company delivery truck.

Opening her front door, she waved to the driver. "Just let me move my car and you can back the truck in here."

She watched with glee as the men unloaded the material for her back deck and they stacked it all up next to the driveway. When the delivery was finished and she was signing the receipt, one of the men commented, "I hope you got help. This is one helluva a project, lady."

"It is! I am so excited to get started." She faced the young man. "I do have help. He's the best!"

Taking her phone out of her back pocket, Laura punched Patrick's number. "Hey, are you ready to put down a back deck?"

"You got your delivery? That was fast." Patrick answered. "How did it go with Vicky?"

"Randy showed up and it wasn't pretty." She explained the confrontation. "Did you set up the call with Randy's daughter, Lisa? When can we do that?"

"In a day or two. I'll let you know. In the meantime, I contacted Debbie Ortega, Donna's coworker and she'll meet with us tomorrow if you like."

"Absolutely. Where are we meeting her?" Laura felt a sense of urgency about this case.

"I thought we could meet in Courthouse Plaza and then go to The Palace where Debbie will be meeting us. What do you think?"

"I think that's perfect. I love that place. They serve great hamburgers. It's fun to see the servers dressed up in period costumes, too." Laura forced her enthusiasm.

"You sound stressed. Are you sure you're alright?" Patrick's sensitivity to her voice and feelings gave Laura pleasure.

"Oh, thanks for that. This is really difficult for me, knowing that my sister's in the worst situation she could be, and I can't do anything about it until we have proof." She added, "I know that sounds selfish because she's the one in the middle of it and I'm on the sidelines looking in at her."

"It's not selfish at all. Look at all you're doing to try and help her." Patrick said. When she didn't reply, he spoke again, "Laura, you're doing everything in your power, but much of this whole ugly mess is out of your control. You've got to realize that!"

Laura hesitated before answering, "When I find myself in this type of situation, I try to have a talk with myself. I have to ask myself if I think better with my heart or my brain? Sometimes the heart wins and other times, the brain takes over. With my sister suffering, my heart is definitely taking over my thoughts."

"I completely understand that. You're an awesome lady and I'm just sorry you're involved in this. Hang in there."

"I will." She seemed to pause but continued, "I can't thank you enough for your help. I wouldn't have had any idea how to investigate this, but with you, it feels like together we can solve this sixteen-year-old murder case."

There was a bit of a silence, not uncomfortable, just thoughtful. "I'll meet you at the statue at noon, okay?" He finally confirmed.

"Yes, I'll be there with bells on. See ya." She hung up. Looking once again at the stack of lumber and building supplies outside, Laura decided she needed some physical relief. Finding her gloves in the small storage room at the back end of her drive, Laura stared at the pile. Reaching for the first box of screws and nails, she hauled them to the back yard.

Little by little, she lifted and carried the boards and other materials that she could handle. She had barely made a dent in the huge pile when she heard her name being called.

"Laura! What in the world are you doing?" Her sister hollered from the open back door.

She wiped the sweat from her forehead as she looked at Vicky. "I'm getting ready to put this deck together. Isn't it going to be grand?" She walked to the back door and stepped onto the temporary blocks to get into the kitchen.

"Ready for a glass of something?" Vicky asked.

"Sure, there's some of that red wine Patrick brought. I have other liquor if you want something stronger." Laura offered.

"Wine is fine. I'll pour."

Laura went to her bathroom and tried to freshen up a bit. She looked at her reflection and noticed several smudges on her face. Immediately, the thought that entered her mind was what would Patrick think if he saw her this way? "Oh, no, we're not going there!" She scrubbed off the dirt and abruptly left the room.

Vicky was sitting at the table, sipping her wine. "Here, I poured you some. Why are you doing all that hard work by yourself? You have a new man in your life. Make him do that heavy work."

Laura looked at her sister, taking her time before responding. "I don't have a new man and you don't have a clue."

Vicky laughed out loud. "Sis, I think you're the one who's clueless. He is a great-looking man and I think he likes you."

"Like I said, you don't know what you're talking about. Patrick is helping with my projects and that's all."

"Why did you divorce Carl?" That question came out of the blue. Vicky waited for her to answer.

"You know that old story."

"I want to know the real reason, please, not the reason you gave everyone else." Vicky pleaded.

"We had grown apart. We both agreed that it was over. Why do you ask?"

Vicky looked her straight in the eyes. "Please, Laura, help me out here. My own marriage is in trouble and maybe if you tell me what went wrong with yours, it'll help me."

"If we're going to have this talk, I'll need more wine." After filling up both of their glasses, Laura sat and started to talk.

"Carl and I hadn't had sex in almost a year. He started sleeping in the other bedroom in the last few months but the thought that suddenly hit me one day was that I didn't care." She sipped her drink before continuing, "Do you understand? We were living like roommates with no benefits, but the worst part was it didn't matter to me. How horrible of a person does that make me?"

"How come you never said anything to me? I thought we were closer than that."

"I'm the big sister and there are certain responsibilities that go with that."

"Bull!" Vicky retorted. "That's just nuts."

Laura took a deep breath. The truth would hurt her sister and accomplish little. Sometimes you lose the battle to win the war. She heard her momma's words in her head. "I guess I just didn't want to burden you with my problems. Carl and I agreed that the marriage was over, and we just had to finish the details and paperwork. It seemed pretty simple at the time, really."

"That sounds so cold. Didn't you love him?" Vicky asked.

"At one time I loved him very much, but as time went on, he worked, and I grew restless. When Josh came along, that helped, but as I grew and matured, it just wasn't enough." Laura recited the facts without much emotion.

"I thought for a while that if we could have a child, it would help, but Randy didn't seem interested." Vicky slipped into reminiscing.

Changing the subject completely, Laura offered, "Hey, how about coming out and helping me finish moving all those supplies to the back yard? I've always found that physical work gets rid of my bad moods."

"You were always so weird!" Her sister replied.

"And you wonder why I didn't talk to you about my problems with Carl and our marriage?" She was already on her feet. "Come on, the work will do you good."

"Ugh! What else bothered you about marriage to Carl?" Vicky didn't move and Laura poured more wine as she sat back down.

"Everything! I hated that he didn't close cupboard doors after he'd been in them, I hated that he left piles of papers on the table, I was tired of waiting for him to get moving when we had to go somewhere. It became a huge game of patience, and mine finally ran out." Laura was still standing there, waiting.

As she poured another glass of wine, Vicky confided as she laughed, "I hate that he sucks his teeth. Instead of getting a toothpick, Randy sits there and tries to suck out whatever is in his teeth."

The sisters couldn't seem to stop their giggling. They continued playing one-upmanship about their husband's annoying habits. With another snicker, Vicky added, "When Randy eats, nothing on his plate can touch anything else. I once served his dinner on one of those divided plates, but he just looked at me. He didn't get it!"

The laughter became more frequent along with the pouring of the wine. "I can remember when all I wanted to do was go out for a drink at the Horny Toad in Carefree, Carl was already in his pajamas."

Vicky's smirk was evident in her voice as well as on her face. "So, what did you do?"

"I packed that sucker up in my car and he went to the bar in his PJ's!" Their laughter grew louder in the small kitchen. Laura couldn't remember the last time they spent as sisters, giggling, drinking and laughing.

"Wait, wait, I can top that. We were invited to a friend's house for a couples dinner. He didn't want to go but instead of telling me that, he just came home late."

"So!"

"I had changed the dinner to take place at our house, and he walked in on four other couples in our dining room." Vicky's laughter stopped her from continuing.

"Come on! What happened?"

"Randy is so worried by what others think, he acted like he had an emergency at the college and there was even a huge bandage on his arm. I think he saw the cars parked in our driveway and put it on to fool our friends. Everyone was so sympathetic that he actually became the hit of the party."

"How did that happen? You worked so hard."

"I know. He's a champion manipulator." Vicky spoke and the laughter was suddenly gone. Vicky stood up, but stumbled a bit. "Let's go outside and move some stuff! I need some fresh air."

On wobbly legs, the two women went out the side door and into the late evening air. "Do you want some gloves?"

"No, I'm fine. You just want to move all this to the back yard?" Vicky pointed to the big pile of construction material.

"Yes."

For the next hour, the two ladies struggled through brains muddled with alcohol, but at the end of their efforts, with satisfaction they saw a huge pile of boards on the back side of the house. "Whew! I didn't think we could do that much."

Vicky agreed with her sister. "I think we should try it without the wine next time!"

Hugging each other, they went back into the house. "Let's eat that leftover spaghetti. Do you realize how much time we spend cooking and eating? Some days it seems that's all I accomplish." Laura got out the leftovers from the refrigerator.

"More wine?" Her sister lifted up her empty glass.

"I think I've had enough for one day. You go ahead if you want, though." Laura said.

Vicky did just that. "What can I do to help?"

"How about some garlic bread to go with this? Everything should be over there in the pantry."

They worked side by side and were soon enjoying a simple meal. As the sisters cleaned up, Vicky asked one more question, "So after all those years with Carl, you just decided enough was enough?"

"I wanted more out of life. So, I threw caution to the wind and divorced him. I moved up here, bought this little old house and have never been happier." She added, "What are you going to do?"

"You mean tonight or with my life?" Vicky asked with a weak attempt at humor.

"Tonight. You don't have to make any other decisions about your life right now. Time will help clear your head."

Vicky hugged Laura, "You're so good. I think I'll go to my bedroom. I just might have a headache to deal with from too much wine."

"Love you." Laura told her.

"Love you, too." She heard Vicky shut her bedroom door.

The night passed quickly. The next morning Laura got ready to meet Patrick at the statue in Courthouse Square, she knew it was too early but found she couldn't contain her excitement. They were ready to interview Donna's best friend, Debbie Ortega from the casino and Laura felt the pressure of time on her shoulders. If they didn't come up with something new and concrete about Randy being a killer, her sister might give in and go back to her husband.

She heard the front door slam shut as Vicky headed out to work at the college. A small smile crossed her face as she thought of the hangover her sister might be experiencing. Her own head wasn't exactly pain-free, but the headache was worth it, she thought. It had been a long time since the two sisters had shared a night of wine and mocking their husband's quirks.

Checking her appearance in the mirror one last time, Laura checked all the doors to make sure they were locked and went out the side door. She looked at the pile of lumber next to her driveway and observed that they had made a sizeable dent in the stack, but there were still a lot of boards that needed to be moved to the back yard. Oh, well, she thought, it gives me something to do tonight.

The drive downtown took her just over ten minutes. Laura decided to go to the Lone Spur and have something for breakfast. She was taken by surprise when her granddaughter greeted her. "Nana! Are you here alone?" Sunny looked around her.

"Yes, who else would be with me?" Laura knew exactly what Sunny was alluding to and wanted to try and avoid any further teasing. "What are you doing here this early?"

"I have late classes today, so I picked up some extra hours. Follow me, you can sit in my section."

After ordering, Laura looked around and noticed that the restaurant wasn't especially busy. This downtown area was usually a livelier spot later in the afternoons. When Sunny brought her the breakfast she ordered, she sat down with her grandmother. "So, what are you and Patrick up to today?"

"What makes you think we're up to something?"

"Nana, really. Lately, you only come to town when you're investigating our case. You're such a homebody."

"If you must know, Patrick and I are going to meet with Debbie Ortega. She worked with Donna at the casino, and they seemed to be good friends."

"Oh, wow, that could be huge. Girlfriends know things that no one else knows. Didn't the police interview her way back when?"

"You have good insight. We're hoping that's the case. Even if they did an interview, they might've missed important clues."

"You'll keep me in the loop?" Sunny stood up as another couple was seated in her section.

"Absolutely, Sunshine. We're a team. Remember?" Laura felt the love for her granddaughter swell in her heart.

"You be safe, Nana. I gotta go."

Laura finished her meal and after leaving a more than generous tip, she walked out into the bright day. On a last-minute impulse, she walked next door into Bashford Courts, one of the small boutique malls surrounding the downtown square whose shops highlight unique gifts and souvenir items for the many visitors to this wonderful western town. Most of the downtown area consists of older buildings converted into smaller shopping malls. Strolling from shop to shop, Laura found several little things she would love to have for her home.

Without making a purchase, she finally left and walked across the busy street to the square. Checking her phone for the time, she saw that she still had about an hour to wait for Patrick. Laura wasn't concerned because she loved to people-watch. Sitting on a bench on the lawn in Courthouse Square enabled her to enjoy her favorite park pastime. She tried to be more observant and notice all the details of people coming and going.

A young couple in the middle of an argument caught her attention, as well as another family trying to keep their young children under control. In front of the statue was a timeline embedded in the concrete showing the history of Arizona. Several different groups of people walked the path, commenting on the information displayed.

During very busy weekends, this same courtyard was filled with various vendors selling their wares, also bands playing on the courthouse steps with lively tunes for all ages. Laura smiled at the satisfaction of living in a simple but lively place.

"What's so funny?"

She heard his voice from behind. The deep tone made her stomach do a few flip-flops, a fact she tried to ignore. "Hello, Patrick. You're early." She didn't answer his question.

"Here, I brought you a coffee, just a teaspoon of sugar, right?"

His thoughtfulness brought more feelings which she chose to disregard. "Thank you. That's nice of you to remember."

"How did things go with you and your sister last night?"

"We drank a lot of wine and then moved part of the lumber pile to the backyard."

Patrick sat down next to her, "Was that a smart thing to do?"

"Do you mean moving the lumber or drinking too much wine?" She teased, knowing full well what he meant.

"That's just like you, wild and crazy. Ready to meet Debbie?" He stood.

"Definitely. The sooner we get concrete information, the sooner I can get my sister away from that maniac." Together they walked across the street to the Palace. Patrick held the door open for Laura and as she entered the darker saloon, she stopped to allow her eyes to adjust. He bumped solidly into her.

"Sorry. I didn't see you stop."

Before she could respond, Laura heard a raspy female voice coming from a table close to the front door. "Patrick! Oh, my God! I know you!"

Eight

An older woman with bleached hair got up and came over to greet them. "When I got your message, the name didn't register, but I wanted to help my old friend. When I saw you come through that door, it all clicked." She gave Patrick a big hug.

"Debbie, this is Laura. She's helping me with this case." Patrick indicated they should get back to the table and extricated himself from her firm hold.

"Nice to meet you. Another detective, huh?" Debbie took a sip of her drink. As early as it was in the day, she didn't seem to have a problem with having a beer.

"Yes, she's been a great help. As I said on my message, we're trying to find out what really happened to Donna."

"So, you're still with the sheriff's office, huh?"

"No, I retired several years ago, after my wife died." He patiently explained.

Laura had to control her urge to burst out laughing as she saw the yearning look on Debbie's face. The woman was definitely interested in the tall, handsome Patrick but he seemed clueless. "Do you want something to drink?" Debbie asked.

They exchanged glances. "No, I'm good. I just had breakfast and drank plenty of coffee." Laura responded.

"I'm good, too."

"Well, how can I help you two?" The older woman looked from one to the other.

"How much do you remember about the night Donna Bell disappeared?" Patrick asked.

"I remember most of it, I think. We were both working, well, almost all the employees were working. It was a holiday weekend, and the town was full of tourists. That's why we all had to park down below in that back lot. Employees were shuttled from our cars to the casino and back when we were finished with our shift."

"Did you ride the same shuttle as Donna?" Laura asked.

"No, I had some paperwork to finish, so I went down on the next one."

"Was she still there?"

"No, but her car was, and I remember thinking that it was weird that she was nowhere around, but her car was there. I just figured her husband or someone else must have picked her up." Debbie sipped on her beer.

"When you say someone, do you mean her boyfriend?" Laura posed the question.

With a slight hesitation, Debbie spoke, "Oh, you know about that? She tried hard to keep it hush-hush. Donna confided in me, but I wasn't sure who else knew about her personal life." Laura noticed Debbie was fidgeting with the bar napkin.

"Did you know who she was seeing? Can you give us a name?" Patrick smiled to soften his question.

"I think you already know him." Debbie seemed reluctant to give up the name of the boyfriend.

Patrick's look of confusion was evident as he prompted her to continue, "Debbie, I'm not sure I know what you mean."

"He worked with you in the sheriff's office. In fact, he was on the team that investigated her disappearance. That's why I thought you would have known about it."

Laura saw by Patrick's demeaner that he was completely stymied. She tried to smooth over his discomfort. "Debbie, are you sure? I'm not familiar with the sheriff's detectives, other than Patrick. Could you please tell me his name?"

"Wayne Houston." Debbie didn't seem to detect the shock she'd just delivered to Patrick. "I never met the man, but Donna was infatuated with him. She talked so much about how nice he was and how he treated her with kindness, not that Randy treated her badly. I just think that her husband pretty much ignored her and any interest from a man who was kind and attentive, was like magic to her."

Patrick finally seemed to snap out of his shock. "You're sure it was Wayne, Wayne Houston?"

"Yeah. She couldn't say enough about how much he treated her with respect. That seemed to be so important to Donna. We were supposed to meet Donna and Wayne, but she disappeared before we could set a date for me and my guy to meet them for dinner. You sure you guys don't want something to drink?" Debbie raised her hand to signal the server.

"Yes, I'll have a beer." Laura was surprised to hear Patrick's response.

After the server came and went, Patrick pressed Debbie for more information. "What else can you tell us about the night Donna disappeared?"

"There's not much more. All I can tell you is that I wasn't surprised. I certainly didn't think she would just go away and I'd never hear from her again. We were friends, you know. Friends keep in contact."

"She never got in touch with you again?" Laura asked.

"Never." Her answer was definitive.

"Is there anything else you can add?" Patrick encouraged her.

Debbie didn't answer right away. "If I think of anything, I'll let you know. Wait, there is one thing I know for sure, Donna would never have left her daughter and she would have contacted her if she could. She was a good mother."

Laura and Patrick stood up and together they went out of the swinging doors of the Palace and into the sunshine. They waited for traffic to clear and then crossed the street over to the courthouse lawn. Neither spoke.

When she heard his voice, Laura finally looked over and faced him. "Let's sit here for a minute."

She hadn't known him long at all, but one thing she knew about this tall man sitting next to her was when he was perplexed, he needed time and space to think. She allowed him that now. The noon sun was lighting up the entire area and she felt the warmth on her face. There was usually a light breeze, and this day was no exception. She watched people strolling, shopping, and enjoying their time in Courthouse Plaza.

"Wow!" He finally spoke. "That was out of the blue!"

"Do you know this person, Wayne Houston?" Her question was redundant. She could tell by his reaction that he did.

"I need to talk with him. He has some explaining to do." His voice showed the anger he was feeling with this new discovery. Patrick turned to face her, "He was on the team investigating Donna's disappearance. Oh my God, did we fail that woman."

"You know what I'm going to say, but I need to tell you anyway. You can't go back and undo what's been done. You are doing the right thing by researching her disappearance now. Nothing has changed. She was missing then, and she's still gone today. You shouldn't beat yourself up."

"I hear your words and I know them to be true, but that doesn't make any of this easier to swallow. I'm going to talk with Wayne Houston. He's still at the sheriff's office."

"Patrick, is that really wise right now?" She challenged his decision as she stood up.

He got up and faced her. "I know you're probably right, but that doesn't mean I have to like it!"

"When I get upset, I need some physical labor to vent my frustrations."

The expression on his face showed confusion. "I don't think I follow."

"How do you feel about putting down my new deck?" She smiled at him.

Patrick chuckled. "I'll meet you at your house. Do you have everything?"

"I am ready for your expertise and help." She gave him a mock salute.

"I'll be right behind you."

"No detours, right?" She wanted to make sure he wasn't going to the sheriff's office, at least for now.

"No, I need to think through my strategy for that one. As far as I'm concerned, Wayne might be a suspect in Donna's disappearance. I wouldn't want to give him a head's up on what I now know."

"Okay, then. See you at the house." She turned to leave but was stopped by his next words.

"Laura, thanks. I think we work well together." With that he walked away, and she stood there pleasantly surprised by his compliment.

Wow, talk about being unexpected, she thought and finally started moving to her own car.

As she pulled into her drive, her cell phone rang. She saw it was her son and answered before getting out of the car. "Hey, son, what's up?"

"I got some good news today and wanted to share." His voice did sound upbeat.

"Did you get that new job?" Laura ventured a guess. "Who is it?"

"Yes! I am so excited. I quit today. I didn't even give those bastards a notice." His laughter was contagious, and she joined in her son's glee. "It's with Embry Riddle, the aeronautical university."

"Good for you. You haven't been happy for a long time."

"Yeah, I'm really looking forward to a new atmosphere. It had gotten so toxic."

"Maybe now you can really use your engineering knowledge. I'm impressed, son. Good for you!"

"Did you talk with Sunny today?"

"As a matter of fact, I saw her this morning. I had to meet Patrick downtown, so I had breakfast before that."

"Oh, so we're still seeing the new man, huh?"

"I'm not 'seeing' anyone. Patrick and I are working on my deck today."

"Need any help?" His offer was shaded with innuendos.

"That's not necessary. Thanks for the offer, though." She giggled, knowing full well what his intentions were.

"Well, Mom, I just wanted to share my good news with you. Have fun working on that deck with your new man. Talk to you later." He rang off before she could reply.

Once out of her car, Laura was just at the side door when she heard Patrick's truck pulling up. Instead of going inside, she turned around to greet him. "See? Vicky and I moved a great deal of lumber the other night, but we hardly touched this pile."

"We'll get it. The boards we need first are those." He pointed to a stack. "Those are the ones that we'll put in as extra porch joists. They'll be strong enough to carry the load for the composite board that goes on top."

"Let me go in and change and then I can start carrying them to the backyard." Before she could move, Patrick picked up several of the heavy boards and headed to the back of her house. She tried to not notice how his arm muscles bulged under the weight of the load he carried with ease.

Going into her house, Laura hurried and changed into her work clothes. As she opened the back door, she could see that Patrick had already started. "What are those?" She pointed to the metal brackets he was nailing to the back wall of her house.

"These are joist hangers. They will support the new beams we're using."

"Can I help?"

"Sure, just come down here and watch me put this one on. Then you can do the same on the other end." Patrick raised his hammer and pounded the nails to hold it securely.

"How do you know if it's level?" She asked.

"Great question. You just need to make sure that this hanger is at the same level as the two on either side of it. I use this level and mark a line at the bottom." He demonstrated the procedure.

"Oh, that seems simple enough. Where do you want me to start?" After some additional explanation, Laura started at the opposite end of the deck. They both worked for an hour or so and soon all the hangers were installed.

"Now what?" She asked.

He looked around at the other side of the deck. "We need to do the same on that side. Ready?"

Determined to keep up with him, Laura went to her side of the deck and started pounding the nails in the hangers. She was working so hard she didn't hear her son's voice until he was practically standing above her. "Mom!"

"Josh! What the hell!" She stood up and looked at Patrick to see his reaction to her son. When no one spoke, she felt compelled to introduce the two. "Patrick, this is my son, Joshua. Josh, this is Patrick. He's helping me with this deck," emphasizing that the only reason Patrick was there was to help with the deck.

Patrick reached out to offer his gloved hand. "Nice to meet you."

"I'm glad to meet my mother's helper. She said she had someone helping with this old deck." Josh grinned.

Even though both men were smiling, Laura knew each was measuring the other for their worthiness in her life. This is ridiculous, she thought suddenly. To her son, "Josh, grab another hammer and help us put these hangers on, no, wait, I have a better idea. Go out front and start bringing back the rest of that lumber. We'll need those 2 X 6 boards first."

Josh laughed and spoke to Patrick, "I hope she doesn't boss you around as much as she does me." When they both laughed, the tension seemed to dissipate between them.

Laura turned back and continued with her task, not waiting to see if the men were working on their projects. The male ego sure is entertaining, she thought to herself. For another hour the three of them worked quietly. Finally, standing up and stretching her aching back, Laura stopped. They had finally finished putting all the brackets on and were ready to install some of the boards.

Patrick put his hammer down and stepped over the framework of the deck. He helped Josh move more of the material to the back yard. Together, they transported almost all the boards. Laura was sitting on a stack of boards when they finally stopped. "Guys! It's time to stop. I'm pooped."

"Hey, Patrick, you want something to drink?" Josh offered.

"Sure, I'll have a beer." He sat down beside Laura. "Bring one for your mother too."

When her son disappeared into the house, Patrick spoke quietly, "We need to go over Wayne Houston's notes with a fine-tooth comb. There might be something there that we can use."

"You mean use against him or use to solve the case?"

"Maybe both." He replied.

They stopped talking when Josh came out with their drinks. Josh joined them, and sat on another pile of boards. "What now? We've still got time to get some of those boards put in place."

"I think I've had enough, son. Thanks for your help, though. Vicky and I started to move those boards, but I'm afraid we didn't get much done."

"Yeah, she told me about your wine fest." He laughed, but on a more serious note. "How do you think she's doing?"

"She's very confused and saddened. I'm not sure what she's going to do in the long run but for now, she's going to stay here with me. What has she said to you about this situation?" Patrick was silent, observing the exchange between Laura and her son.

"We talked just last night, and I agree with you. Vicky is mixed up and very unsure of her future. She finally told me that she thinks Randy has a shady past."

"What do you think she meant?" Laura asked her son.

He looked at Patrick before answering. "I think you know more about this, you and Patrick here."

"You're as smart as your mother, Josh." Patrick finally joined the conversation. "We are very worried for Vicky. She's in serious trouble and all we want to do is help her."

"What do you want from me?" Josh looked directly at Patrick and when neither one of them responded quickly, he added, "I'm serious, how can I help?"

Patrick waited for Laura to answer that one. "I think, and Patrick, correct me if you think I'm wrong, but the best thing for you to do right now is just to be there for Vicky."

"That seems so useless. Can't I help investigate?" Joshua seemed eager to help with the details.

"It's a slow process. It's not like in the movies, but I appreciate your offer. If there's anything we need, we'll let you know." Patrick looked to Laura for confirmation.

"I agree. Vicky trusts you and if you learn anything that you think might be of value to us, just let us know."

"In the meantime, son, don't let her know how much is going on behind the scenes. She's in such a tizzy as it is, and we don't need her going off the deep end." Laura said.

"I agree, but if you think of something else, let me know, Mom." Joshua said.

"Will do. Now, how about something to eat? It's almost time for dinner." Laura offered.

"Nah, I've got to get home and check on Sunny. She's always on the run, but I make sure she checks in with me so I know she's okay." He stood up and extended his hand. "Patrick, nice to meet you. You've got your work cut out for you, keeping this one in check."

"You watch your mouth, son!" Laura laughed at her son's joke as he disappeared around the corner.

"Can he be trusted?" She heard Patrick's question.

"Of course, he's my son!" She got up and started heading to the back door. "Are you hungry?"

"How about just some snacks? I want to go over Wayne Houston's notes, and we can do that together. I'm not very hungry."

"Come on, then. We'll go to the office, so that we can keep our notes from prying eyes. You go on in there and I'll bring something to snack on."

Laura walked through the office door with a tray of food and saw that Patrick had settled down in the chair behind her desk. He was poring over the notes from his old files. She hated to disturb his thought process and tried to move quietly.

"Hey, thanks." He moved some papers from the corner of the desk to make room for the tray. "I've been going over these notes and so far, I can't find anything out of whack."

"Here, have something to eat and I'll look." She pulled the papers over to the other side of the desk as she sat on the extra chair.

She read with meticulous intention each note written by Wayne Houston. Finally, Laura went back and reviewed each page until Patrick finally cleared his throat. "Anything?"

"Yes, but let me go over it again before I say anything."

She looked over and waited just a moment before speaking, "Patrick, you're a seasoned detective, right?"

"Yes."

When she didn't react, he prompted, "Laura, what's your point?" His frustration was evident in his voice as he stood up and came around to look over her shoulder. "What did you find?"

"Give me another minute, okay?" She kept staring at the paper in front of her, but finally looked up only to come nose to nose with Patrick. His closeness startled her, but she quickly regained her composure and leaned back.

Handing him the document she'd been studying, Laura threw out her challenge. "When you look at this, I mean really look, what exactly do you see?"

"If I knew that, we wouldn't be having this conversation. Spill it, lady. What obvious thing have I missed?"

Laura giggled a little but saw that his frustration level was rising, and she quickly answered him. "This was Wayne's interview with Randy but if you look more closely, he didn't ask any pertinent questions. Patrick, this should be several pages long, not just two!"

A thoughtful look passed over his face as realization dawned on him. "You are so right!" He reread the questions and answers listed on the report and handed it back to her. "What else?"

"The first question Wayne asked Randy was 'where were you the night your wife disappeared?', and Randy said he was home sleeping. His follow-up question was 'can anyone confirm that'. Randy said their daughter was at home too."

"What else should he have asked?" Patrick was more relaxed and grinning by this time.

Laura felt herself relax as he moved back behind the desk. This man was starting to work on her emotions. As that thought crossed through her being, she realized that their relationship was becoming more important with each contact and that was not what she had planned for her future.

"Laura! What didn't Wayne Houston ask of Randy?" Patrick repeated his question.

"Sorry, I took a side trip there." She shifted in her chair. "He should have asked him why it took him so long to report that Donna was missing. Another problem is that Randy didn't call from home, he drove to the parking lot and called the police from there. Don't you think that's weird? Why didn't he call the casino and ask for her?"

"What do you think the lack of information in his report means?"

"Now that you and I have found out that Donna was seeing this detective, the lack of information here tells me that he already knew the answers and chose not to ask the questions. Where is the interview with their daughter?"

Patrick sorted through the stacks of papers and finally pulled out the document. "There isn't much here either. She was thirteen at the time and somewhat clueless about the whole situation, a typical teenager."

When Laura finished looking over the sheet, she looked up and their eyes met. "I'm sorry but I just have to ask. Where are the interviews you conducted?"

Once again, Patrick shuffled through the information and handed several documents to her. Laura took several long minutes reading them. "See, this just proves my point. Look at how much detail you put into these reports. I have no unanswered questions."

"Aww, shucks, ma'am. You're just being kind." His response of mock embarrassment made her laugh.

"All this makes me wonder about the interview we're going to have with Lisa, Randy and Donna's daughter. Did you get that scheduled yet?"

"As a matter of fact, she's going to text me tomorrow and we'll follow up with a video chat. You and I should be together so we both can be participating. I could come over and work on the deck again if you'd like."

"I would never turn down extra help. I didn't realize how big this project was going to be. Should we work on our questions for Lisa?"

After he agreed, they worked for another hour until Patrick stood up and stretched. "I think it's time for me to go home. We got a lot done, don't you think?"

"Yes, we did. Thanks so much for the work on my deck. I know I would still be hauling the boards from the front to the back. With help from you and Josh, I know it won't be long before we can enjoy a great barbeque out there. I'll walk you out."

On the way out, he grabbed his cowboy hat from the kitchen counter and put it on. She found herself becoming familiar with his routines, another thought that disturbed her. Just as he was at the front door, her cell phone rang with Joshua's ring tone.

She put up her finger to indicate Patrick should wait. "Josh, what's up?"

"Can you send Sunny home?"

"She's not here, otherwise I would. I saw her at work this morning but haven't heard from her since." A little tight feeling in her stomach warned

Laura that something wasn't right. "Did you call her? Of course, you did. That was silly of me. I'll try and call you back."

"What's going on with Sunny?" Patrick deduced what the conversation had been about.

"Josh hasn't heard from her and that's unusual. She's always calling one of us and she's good at keeping in touch." As she was talking, Laura called Sunny's number. "It went straight to voice mail. Something's not right, Patrick. With everything she knows, I'm concerned."

"You don't think she'd try to do some detecting on her own, would she?" Patrick asked.

The look on Laura's face confirmed what they were both thinking. "Where do we start looking for her?"

"Get in my truck and we'll drive by Randy's house. From there, I don't have any idea, but we can think on the way." She got her purse and locked the front door.

"I'll send her some texts and hopefully, she'll respond. Then we'll both beat her up." Laura's voice shook with fear.

Despite the urgency of their trip, Patrick drove carefully and safely. Neither spoke. The trip from Laura's place to Randy's house wasn't far. Although tourists were the main source of income, the price the townspeople paid was the busy car and pedestrian traffic.

As they drove up Lee Boulevard, Laura was grateful that the small, rural atmosphere in the suburb didn't allow for streetlights. Patrick's truck wouldn't be seen by anyone at the house as they drove by. Continuing slowly up the winding street, they were both straining to see any sign of Sunny's car. The lights were on at Randy's house, but her granddaughter's vehicle was not there.

"What now?" She asked.

"Let's just circle around the neighborhood, maybe we'll get lucky." There was virtually no traffic this time of night so Patrick could drive slowly without being in the way. He started to turn right when she stopped him. "Go up to that house where we were the other day. Maybe Sunny found it and wanted to observe the house. She's a very smart girl, maybe too smart for her own good."

"Oh, my God! There's her car." Patrick had barely stopped his truck before Laura jumped out. She ran over and looked inside. "She's not here. Where could she be?"

Patrick tried to open the car door, but it was locked. He went back to his truck and got a flashlight. As they both peered in, they could see Sunny's purse and her phone on the seat. "Damn! What in the world did she think she was doing?"

"I can't see down below on the hillside. It's too dark."

Patrick again went to the truck and came back with night-vision binoculars. He scoured the area between them and Randy's house. "Do you see anything?" Laura's voice was tinged with worry.

Just then they both noticed the lights were turned off in the house and the headlights on Randy's truck came on. He backed out of his driveway and disappeared down the street. "Come on." Patrick spoke abruptly.

Once in the truck, they drove back down the hill and were soon in Randy's driveway. "What if he comes back?" Laura was in a panic.

"No worry, here's our little girl now." Patrick pointed to Sunny, who was running out to them.

Patrick called out to Sunny, "Get in!" As fast as he could, drove the opposite way to get out of the subdivision.

"Before you yell, Nana, I have some great information for you two." Sunny's words were laced with a mixture of fear and pride.

Nine

"Sunshine Marie Shepherd, you are in the absolute deepest trouble you've ever been in!"

"Oh, man, she never uses my full name." The tiny voice came from the back seat of the truck.

Patrick had to contain a chuckle as he chose to stay out of the line of fire between grandmother and granddaughter. The silence in the truck was thick with tension, but he knew once they got back to Laura's home, all hell might break loose. Sunny kept silent, a wise move on her part. Patrick noticed Laura texting on her phone and assumed it was to Josh to let him know they had found her and she was safe.

"Patrick, take me up to her car. We need to get it home."

Once up at the lot above Randy's house, he pulled in behind Sunny's little car. "Come on." Laura ordered her granddaughter.

"I think I'd rather ride with Patrick." When Laura looked around, she saw Sunny sitting there with her arms crossed and a look of attempted defiance on her pretty young face. Laura looked at Patrick and saw his nod.

"Fine, but it's only going to delay the inevitable." She held her hand out for the car keys. Once Sunny gave them to her, she shut the door and soon they were all on the road. Laura wondered what the conversation was like between Patrick and her errant granddaughter. She felt she knew him well enough by now that he would take the opportunity to support their stand about Sunny going off on a dangerous stunt.

She saw with chagrin that Vicky's car was in the driveway. This meant that any conversation between Sunny and herself would be delayed even further. Entering the kitchen, she noticed her sister was sitting at the table, drinking wine and snacking on cheese and crackers. "Hey, how's it going?" Vicky greeted her.

"Oh, it's going. How are you doing?" Laura got another glass from the wine rack and poured herself a drink.

"I'm fine. I noticed you got more work done on the deck. It's going to look great. Did Patrick help?"

"Yes, and Josh came over too. It's a bigger project than I realized and I don't think I could've gotten it done without their help."

Just then the door opened and Patrick and Sunny came in. She hoped that Vicky wouldn't feel the tension between them. "Hey, you two! What are you all doing?"

Patrick supplied the answer. "Sunny needed a ride here and I was in the area, so I volunteered."

"What's for dinner?" Vicky asked.

"I'm going to head home. I've got a meeting with a client in the morning, and I need to finish some information on the proposal." Patrick volunteered.

"I need to get home too. Dad will be waiting for me to help with dinner." Sunny hoped her answer would get her out of the lecture she knew was yet to come.

Realizing the need for secrecy, Laura agreed. "Patrick, call me when you get time and Sunny, I'll see you in the morning, first thing."

As quick as she could, Sunny came over and gave her grandmother a kiss on the cheek. "I love you, Nana."

The look Laura gave Sunny spoke volumes. "I love you too, Sunshine. Please come over early and we'll have breakfast." She hoped Sunny would get the subliminal message as she rubbed her hand over her nose. It had been their secret signal to let each other know to keep moving on, or that there was a problem, without saying a word.

"I'll be here first thing, promise," and out the door she went.

Patrick gave a small salute to both women and soon they were left alone in the kitchen. "How come I feel like I am in the middle of a movie? What's going on, Sis?"

"Oh, you know how teenagers can be. Sunny needed her car brought home. I think she just panicked."

"I do know how that can be, I know nothing when my car doesn't work right. Randy is always having to fix the little things. At least your man was handy and could help her." Vicky grinned when she saw the look of disgust on Laura's face.

"He's not my man!" After seeing the smile on her sister's face, she added, "He's a very nice man, but we're only working together. There's nothing personal at all."

"Protest all you want; I see the sparks that fly between you two."

"What do you want for dinner?" Laura went to the refrigerator and opened the door to view the possibilities.

Vicky came up and hugged her sister, "I love you. You are so cute when you get embarrassed. Let's just have something simple. I already had a big lunch."

The rest of the night passed quietly as both women seemed preoccupied with their own thoughts and problems. Finally, Vicky announced she was going to bed, leaving Laura to clean up the kitchen and settle down in her own bedroom. Thoughts of Sunny's carelessness was prominent on her mind as she settled down in bed.

Her dreams weren't pleasant but as the sun streamed into her room the next morning, Laura woke up prepared ready to deliver the stern talk her granddaughter needed.

Switching the coffee maker on, she read the note her sister left. "Hey, might be late tonight. Don't wait on me for dinner."

Laura started frying bacon as she drank a cup of the freshly-brewed coffee. As she put the last of the bacon strips on the platter, she heard the rather timid knock at her kitchen door. "Come on in, Sunny."

Her beautiful granddaughter came right in and hugged her grandmother tightly. "Nana, I'm so sorry I worried you two, but I really found out some great information."

"How many eggs would you like?"

"I'll have scrambled." Sunny helped herself to a cup of coffee and sat down at the table.

As they sat down together to eat their breakfast, Laura finally asked her, "What happened that made you decide to put yourself in danger?"

"Nana, I was serving two guys after you left the restaurant when I overheard them saying something about Uncle Randy, so I decided to listen closely."

When Laura didn't say anything, Sunny continued without prompting. "I heard them say that they were going to Uncle Randy's house to plan a new job. They talked about stuff being worth thousands of dollars! Nana, I heard them say they were meeting at his house later in the evening and then were going to some storage room. I didn't have time to make a decision other than to get more information. I knew I needed to help you and Patrick get some evidence."

"What did you do then?"

"When I got off work and went to Uncle Randy's house and no one was there, I used the key that Aunt Vicky kept under the flowerpot. Do you remember that voice-activated recorder you got me for school? Well, I thought that any meeting would probably be in the kitchen, so I taped the recorder underneath the table.

Working hard to contain her pride in Sunny's deductions and clear thinking, Laura waited for her to finish the story. "So, what happened then?"

"I left as fast as I could so no one would catch me there. My hands were shaking and my stomach was in knots. I guess I should have called you then, but I had to go to school and time flew by. Before I knew it, I was done with class and I wanted to go back and get that recorder before someone else discovered it."

"You still should have called me. Sunny, this is not something I want you involved in at all, let alone putting yourself in the path of a dangerous man! We are not playing games here. I know you think of him as just Uncle Randy, but everyone has a past and his could be deadly."

Sunny got up from the table and came around to give her grandmother a tight hug. "I love you and I know you think I'm an innocent young girl, but Nana, I think I'm able to take care of myself."

The repetitive knock on the kitchen door indicated that Patrick was there. His presence filled the room. Patrick appeared freshly showered as he removed his Stetson and placed it on the breakfast bar, his dark hair shining with moisture. Laura had to stop herself from staring. "Hey, ladies, what's happening? I see you're still alive and well, Sunny." He grinned as he spoke to her.

Sunny stood up and hugged him. "I'm sorry that I made you worry. Nana can bring you up to date." He gave her a tight squeeze back.

Laura got up and offered him a cup of coffee as she explained where they were in the story. Sunny started the rest of her tale when they were all seated around the table. "I went back to Uncle Randy's and there weren't any cars, but I just had a feeling that it was close to the time when they were to meet, so I went to that lot above his house and waited."

Looks passed between Laura and Patrick, which didn't go unnoticed by Sunny. "I know what you two must be thinking, but I was being very sure and safe. I didn't go down to Uncle Randy's house until I saw them all leave."

"Oh, my God, Sunny. Do you realize that this is a very dangerous situation?" Patrick posed the question.

"I've already gotten that lecture from Nana! You two need to learn how to chill!" Sunny rolled her eyes.

Patrick avoided looking at Laura when he answered Sunny. "What did you do then?"

"Once they left, I climbed down that damn...darn hill and up the other side to get that recorder before they all came back!" Her impatience was showing. "I went in the house and got the recorder from under the table when I heard their cars pulling in. I ran to that front coat closet; you know the one with extra space in the side?"

"Oh, my God, Sunny! What were you thinking?" Patrick nearly exploded.

With a huff, she answered, "What else did you expect me to do? I didn't want them to catch me."

"Okay, okay, what happened then?" Laura tried to calm everyone down.

"They went to the kitchen table and talked for a few minutes, not long. Before you ask, I couldn't hear them through the door. As soon as I heard the front door slam, I waited long enough to know that I was alone for a moment, and I hurried out. That's when I saw you two and dashed!"

There was silence as each of them digested the situation on their own terms. Finally, Patrick asked, "Did you listen to the tape?"

With a sly smile, Sunny replied, "What do you think?"

They all laughed and the tension in the room finally broke. "Am I forgiven?" She gave an innocent smile with her request.

In unison, they both replied, "No!"

"What? I can't believe you two! I know that I acted impulsively, but I have great information. I am sitting here safe and sound, so no harm!"

"You say, 'no harm' Sunshine, but we were worried sick about you. I know he's your uncle, but he could be a killer. I've seen things that would curdle your blood. Don't ever underestimate the enemy!" Patrick was emphatic.

"You keep saying that, and I truly believe that you've been involved in some terrible situations, but Patrick, I have only seen crime shows on television. I can't even imagine that my uncle would be involved in something as horrific as that."

"Let me tell you one thing, Sunny, someone who has killed before will not hesitate to do it again!" Patrick got up from the table. "I think I need to go."

Laura stood up, "Please wait. We haven't heard the tape. Let's all calm down and listen."

Sunny stood up and went to him, "Please, Patrick, listen to the recording. I don't mean to upset you, please."

With a deep breath, he came back to the table and sat down. "We need to finish this investigation and this tape, although illegal, is important. Sunny, you must promise your grandmother and me that you will not do such a dangerous thing again!"

"I promise!" She raised her hand.

"Let's listen." Laura tried to change the direction of their conversation.

Sunny pushed the button on the small recorder and together they heard three men talking. The recording was a bit garbled but three distinct voices came through. Patrick, Laura and Sunny remained silent for the first run-through of the audio tape. As soon as it was finished, Laura spoke, "What do you think?"

Patrick replied, "I know the voice of Randy, but do either of you know the other two?"

"If it means anything, when I saw these guys at the restaurant, I didn't recognize either of them."

"It definitely sounds like they're planning another burglary, doesn't it?" Laura volunteered.

Just as Patrick was about to reply, his phone buzzed. He looked at the message. "Laura, we have our video meeting in just a little while. We may need to finish this later."

"I have to get to class anyway. Are you two no longer mad at me?" Sunny stood up, ready to leave.

Patrick looked to Laura for direction. Laura simply said, "I don't know what to say!"

"I've heard a picture is worth a thousand words." Patrick searched for a certain picture on his phone. "Sunny, I don't mean to shock you, but this young lady believed she could handle any situation, too." He held out his phone, but before showing the screen to her, he prompted, "You don't have to look, you can just trust me that bad things can happen to good people."

Curiosity got the best of her, and Sunny leaned over to see the picture on his phone. She didn't have to look long, "OMG! What happened to her?"

Patrick offered his phone to Laura, but she declined to look at it. "It was one of the cases that I hated most. This young girl was about your age when she decided that dating a guy against her parents' wishes was what she wanted to do. To make a long story short, she was found in the woods out by Lynx Lake. The killer made sure she suffered a long and painful death."

"Don't you think it's kinda creepy to have a picture like that on your phone?" Sunny's question was blunt.

"Sure it is, but if this kind of picture stops one person from making a deadly decision, then I guess I'm guilty of being creepy. I've told both of you before, neither of you have any idea how gruesome and cruel it can be in my world."

"Okay, I get it! I won't make any more questionable decisions without letting you two in on it. Here, give me your phone." As she took it from Patrick, she put in her number. "Text me and I'll have your number. I can guarantee you both that I'll not be doing any more detective work on my own anymore."

"Sunny, we'll take you at your word." Laura hugged her before she left the room.

Turning to Patrick, Laura apologized, "I'm sorry, she's seventeen going on thirty."

Without thinking, Patrick drew her close in a big hug. "I was a teenager once, believe it or not. I hope I wasn't too hard on her."

His touch felt good, too good, she thought but didn't pull back. Finally, Laura stepped out of his embrace. "If it saves her from harm, I'm all for it."

"Let's go to your office and make some notes before the call with Randy's daughter." He grabbed his phone, not waiting for her to follow. Laura was right behind him with freshly filled coffee cups.

"Can you fire up your computer? I'm hoping Lisa will keep her commitment to talk with us, but I don't want any technical glitches to cause us problems. Thanks for this." He raised his coffee cup in salute.

Together they worked to prepare for a call they desperately hoped would come. Patrick busied himself making notes in the notebook he always carried. Laura had the computer on and was online, waiting for any indication that their video conference call was active.

The wall clock indicated that the time for their meeting had come and gone. "Maybe Lisa changed her mind." Laura offered her opinion. She looked up as Patrick stood over her shoulder looking at the screen.

"We'll give it another five minutes or so."

The silence was heavy between them as Laura tapped nervously on the keyboard, randomly searching the internet. A small beep on the screen stopped them both. "This is it."

A face appeared on the screen and a young woman introduced herself, "Hello. I'm Lisa." If she was nervous, it didn't show. Laura studied the screen, trying to find clues, any indication that might help them.

"Hello, Lisa. I'm Patrick and this is Laura. We're so glad you agreed to talk with us."

"I was curious. It's been sixteen years, and I did everything I could to get away from that horrible situation." Lisa took a moment to gather her composure.

"I just want you to know that we appreciate you taking our call. This must be difficult for you." Patrick used his best 'I'm on your side' voice. "Would you mind if we record this call? It would help us as we review our notes later."

"Nothing has been easy since my mother died, so go ahead."

"May I ask you a question?" Laura finally spoke up.

"Sure." Lisa shrugged her shoulders.

"I miss my mom every day since she died. What do you remember most about your mother?" Laura asked.

With a small smile, Lisa answered, "She was the best cook. I loved her surprise meals. She was so creative; she could have been a great chef."

"Do you cook too?" Laura was encouraged to continue by the slight pressure on her shoulder from Patrick's hand.

"I do my best but I'm not as good as I remember my mom was in the kitchen. My husband likes what I cook, so I guess that counts." Again, there was a shrug of her shoulders. "I have a question for you."

"Ask away." Laura answered.

"Why are you two interested in my mother's disappearance after all these years? Are you detectives?"

Laura looked at Patrick as he took the chair next to her. "I was one of the original investigators on her case." He waited for that information to soak in before continuing. "I am now retired but I have never forgotten about your mother."

"And you?" Lisa asked Laura.

Oh, how much do I tell her? Laura's thoughts were flying around in her head. Before she could answer, Patrick spoke for her, "Laura's my techy help. I'm no good at these computer things."

"Oh, I totally understand that. I'm just barely able to get by on the computer." Lisa finally showed a bit of nervousness as there was a quiet moment.

"Lisa, how much do you remember about the day your mother went missing?" There. Patrick got to the heart of their meeting.

"On one hand, over the years, I find myself forgetting more and more, but then some little memory will unexpectedly pop into my head. There was a lot of confusion with people coming and going during that time. Police questioned my dad for days." She spoke softly.

"Your mother has never contacted you?" Laura asked.

"No. We've never heard a word from her. I was finally sent back east to live with my aunt, my dad's sister."

"What's a little memory that popped into your head recently?" Patrick pursued that topic.

Lisa shifted in her seat, her discomfort visible. "Suddenly, I remembered a conversation with my mom just before she disappeared." Lisa stopped and appeared to be collecting her thoughts. "She picked me up from school, which is something she didn't normally do. Once I was in the car, mom announced that we were going shopping for some clothes for me."

"Why did that seem out of the ordinary?" Laura asked.

"Like I said, she hardly ever picked me up from school without it being a planned event. Just a few months before, when the school year started, we had gone shopping and bought me a lot of new clothes. I didn't really need anything."

"I guess I don't understand. What do you think it meant?" Patrick pretended ignorance.

"I think my mom knew she wasn't going to be there and wanted me to have enough clothes so I wouldn't have to depend on my dad for that. You know how men don't think of that sort of thing."

"I get that. My granddaughter depends on me and not her dad for clothes shopping." Laura commented. "Lisa, what was the atmosphere in the house before she left? I mean, were your mom and dad getting along?" She noticed Patrick's nod of approval of her question.

"Oh, that's a question the cops asked me back then. As a thirteen-year-old, I told them they were getting along."

"But? I feel you might have a different answer now." Patrick stated.

"This is not easy to talk about. I lost not only my mother but my father back then. My whole world became a nightmare!" She was visibly upset.

"Take a minute if you need to, Lisa." Laura encouraged her.

"Excuse me for a minute." Lisa got up and they were left staring at an empty chair.

Patrick wrote some notes and Laura stared at the screen, both patiently waiting and hoping Lisa would return to finish their interview.

Just when they thought she might not come back, Lisa appeared and sat back down in the well-worn leather desk chair. "I'm sorry about that. Someone was at the door."

"We can't thank you enough, Lisa. We can only imagine how hard this is for you." Laura tried some comforting words to put the younger woman at ease.

"You know, I just want some closure to this whole nightmare. Nothing, absolutely nothing will make everything all right, but to find out exactly what happened would go a long way to giving me some peace in my life. To answer your question from earlier, I thought my mom and dad were just normal parents, but thinking back on it, they were fighting a lot. They were both unhappy and it wasn't that they fought so much, it was that they just started living their own, separate lives."

"Do you think they were seeing other people?" Patrick asked.

"I think my mom was, but my dad spent so much time at work, I don't think he had any idea of what was really going on in the house. He was always at work. Maybe my mom was bored. I was just thirteen. It was a disaster waiting to happen." Suddenly, Lisa stared at the screen, "You know this has been harder than I thought it would be. I'm done."

"Oh, okay. We are so grateful that you took the time to talk with us." Patrick barely got his words out when Lisa ended the call.

"Wow! I don't know about you, but I think that went better than I expected." Laura looked over at him.

"I'll have to digest everything that she said. I'm glad she agreed to the recording, even if she was reluctant."

"I think I need to get some work done. What are you going to do?" Laura stood up and stretched her back.

"Are you working on the deck?" He asked.

"Yes, I am anxious to get it finished."

"I'll help." He followed her out the back door.

Together they spent several hours putting more boards on the deck. It was starting to come together, and she could at least walk out the back door without falling. They hadn't discussed the call at all. It was as if both were trying to evaluate the interview on their own.

Finally, Laura sat down and announced, "I'm pooped! I'm sure you have other things to do and as much as I appreciate your help, I don't want to keep you from your other jobs."

"Are you trying to get rid of me?" He sat next to her.

"Not at all, but I know this case has consumed a lot of your time."

"Laura, if I needed to be somewhere else, I'd let you know. I agreed to help you, but I also wanted answers for myself."

They sat there with the sun shining above and silence between them. Finally, Patrick cleared his throat, "Laura, I do have something to do, but first I'd like to ask you a question."

"Sure, ask away."

"How about we go out and have a nice dinner later?"

"Dinner? Us?" She questioned him. The surprise must have shown on her face. "Oh, I guess you want to talk about Lisa's interview today. That sounds like a good idea."

"No, no, I would like to get to know you better. I've enjoyed being with you, but we've been so busy with this case and working on the deck, I just think it's about time I learned what makes you tick." He stood and offered her a hand up.

His touch did send a tingle through her hand. "You mean a date, a real date?"

After seeing Patrick nod his head, Laura smiled and agreed. "Okay, I think that might be a good idea. Where should I meet you?"

"You're an independent cuss, aren't you?" He responded.

"I should think you would have figured that out by this time."

His laughter warmed her heart. When they walked back to the kitchen, Patrick grabbed his Stetson, placing it on his head. "How about you meet me at Murphy's around six?"

"That sounds great."

As she watched him pull away from the curb, Laura found herself grinning. Walking back into the house, she sent a text to her sister. "Guess what? I have a date."

Vicky replied, "Really? The cowboy finally got brave enough to ask?"

"Who do you think it is?"

"Patrick, of course! Sis, you can be so silly. I know you two have been attracted to each other since the beginning. Have fun! See you later!"

Ten

Laura took one last look in the mirror, giggling as she remembered one of her daddy's favorite sayings. In her mind she could hear his gravelly voice say she was as nervous as a long-tail cat in a room full of rocking chairs. She took a deep breath before speaking to her reflection, "It's just a meal with a new friend, remember that's all you want!"

The drive to Murphy's didn't take long at all, parking took more time as this restaurant was very popular any time of the week. The site itself began in 1890 as a general mercantile store and its character was prevalent in the building's exterior. Walking into the restaurant was like taking a step back in time with the two-story building alive with conversation. The dark mahogany banister led to the upper dining area with its crown molding and metal-tiled ceiling. She could envision gas light sconces on the side walls giving a soft romantic glow to the room.

Above the bar were shelves displaying merchandise from days of old with a library-type ladder that allowed the merchant to move from left to right to gather items for the costumer.

Glancing to her left, she saw Patrick leaning against the bar. He was staring at her and their eyes locked. Without realizing it, she was already by his side. His hat was on the bar, allowing him to lower his head and place a tender kiss on her lips. "Wow, that was nice." She spoke softly.

"We have a little time before a table opens. Would you like something to drink?" Patrick pulled out the stool next to his.

"I'd like another kiss first."

Without hesitation, he kissed her again, but this time it was more than a tender little kiss.

Breathlessly, she spoke, "Now, I'll have that drink." Patrick helped her up on the bar stool.

Patrick signaled the bartender, and Laura ordered a glass of wine. He indicated a refill for his own drink and turned to smile at Laura. "Okay?"

"I'm fine. I like this."

"A little unsettling?" His question mirrored her own thoughts.

"Yes and no. I think we can agree that there has been an attraction between us from the beginning, can't we?" She eagerly sipped her drink.

"You know, that's one of the things I've come to appreciate about you the most."

"What's that?" She looked at him and felt herself lost in his beautiful brown eyes.

"Your honesty and your ability to get right to the point." He leaned over and put his hand over hers.

"Dad?" They both turned to face the pretty woman standing before them.

Patrick jumped to his feet and hugged his daughter. "Laura, this is my daughter, Sharon."

Laura stood up and took her outstretched hand. "It's nice to meet you."

"Laura is the woman I've told you about. I'm helping her with a cold case."

"Oh, yes, I do remember you saying something about that. How's it going?"

"We're making some progress." Patrick's answer was deliberately vague.

His daughter looked at Laura, "That's what my dad says when he doesn't want to divulge top-secret information." Her smile was genuine, making Laura feel more comfortable.

"What are you doing here?" Patrick asked.

"I just finished a meal with some of my coworkers. We decided that we needed a treat."

"Where do you work?" Laura asked.

"I sell insurance. It's a small office, but we're a tight bunch and need celebrations often."

"Will you join us for a drink?" Laura asked.

"No, I've had enough and need to get home. It was nice to meet you. Have fun." Sharon kissed her dad on the cheek and left in a hurry as she waved at them both.

"She seems very nice." Laura spoke.

"Sharon's a great daughter. She works hard but I'm hoping she and her husband will decide to finally give me a grandchild." His pride was evident.

"Do you think she was surprised to see us here?" Laura asked.

"I'm sure she was, but not in a negative way. She's always told me that I should start dating again." Patrick answered honestly.

"How sweet." At that moment, the host indicated their table was ready and led them up the stairs to a table overlooking the floor below. Once their server had taken their dinner order, Patrick raised his glass to toast.

"Here's to getting to know each other better."

"I have a question for you." She waited for him to respond. Once she saw him smile, Laura continued, "Why did you become a detective?"

"Oh, wow, that's not what I expected." He waited for their fresh drinks to appear before answering. "It's not a complicated story. I'm not the son of a cop and there's no history to live up to in the family. As a kid in school, I liked solving problems. On career day in seventh grade, the father of one of my classmates came and spoke. He was a detective for the FBI, and I guess that's all she wrote."

"That's awesome! Isn't it amazing how one interaction can form our path in life?" She leaned back as the server placed their salads on the table.

"I have a question but it's rather personal." He looked to see her reaction.

"Go for it."

"You told me that you married at the tender age of fifteen and you weren't pregnant. Why? What did your parents have to say about that? I mean, it's obvious they didn't stop you."

"No, they didn't. In fact, my mom had to go before a judge to get permission because of my age." She hesitated but continued. "I grew up very poor. My dad was hit and miss in our lives, and my mom could barely make ends meet. We lived in the projects in Avondale. I think it was almost relief on her part when I wanted to leave, you know, one less mouth to feed."

Enjoying their salads while contemplating the information just shared, the din of conversation around them helped to dispel any tension. "It's amazing, isn't it? Take, for example, the fact that we connected because of your sister's troubles."

With a small frown on her face, Laura agreed. "I only hope we can solve this before something terrible happens."

He reached over and placed his hand over hers. "Let's not think about anything negative tonight, okay?"

"You're right. I think we both needed a little break, and this is great. Thank you."

As the waiter appeared with their dinner, Laura sat back and enjoyed the moment. "Mmm, this looks yummy."

They took their time, savoring every bite. There seemed to be no need for conversation as a comfortable atmosphere settled over them. Finally, Laura pushed back her plate. "I couldn't possibly eat any more. That was delicious."

"I'm with you. This steak was cooked perfectly but I think I'll have some to take home for lunch tomorrow." He smiled at her.

"I'll have mine for lunch tomorrow, too. Maybe I'll enjoy it out on my new patio deck. It's almost finished, and I can't thank you enough. I didn't realize it was going to be such a huge project. Josh is a good helper, but he has things to do in his own life and can't always be there for me. I feel like I should pay you for your work."

"You're so welcome, Laura, don't even think about paying me. Just consider it a friend helping a friend."

"I really want you to know how much I appreciate it." Just then the server came up to ask about dessert.

After declining any more food and boxing up the leftovers, Patrick asked. "They're having some music in the plaza tonight. Want to go and listen?"

"That sounds good. I could use a little walk right now."

She felt his hand on her back as they walked up the block to Courthouse Plaza. Laura heard the strains of country music which grew louder as they got closer to the plaza. The grounds were crowded with people enjoying the evening concert. Some were sitting on blankets and others were on the benches.

"This is one of the things I love most about this little town. There always seems to be something to do, and lots of times it doesn't cost a dime." She smiled at him.

"It's not such a little town anymore. The population seems to grow an average of over two hundred thousand people a year. I think we're the 23rd largest city in the state now."

"How in the world would you know that?"

"As a member of the law enforcement community, you learn to keep track of certain statistics. When Prescott was a small town, the crime rates reflected the population. We had the occasional murder but now with the increase in people, the crime rates are definitely getting worse."

She reached over and patted his arm. "You certainly look at the world from different eyes, don't you?"

"Look around and tell me what you see." He encouraged Laura.

She did as he asked. "I see lots of happy people, some enjoying the music, some enjoying each other but most of them are having fun. What are you looking at?"

Patrick pointed over to a young mother sitting on a blanket holding her little child. "See that woman? Look behind her and tell me what's there."

Laura stared at the scene and suddenly saw what he was referring to as she noticed a rather scruffy young man just beyond the blanket. "He seems out of place, doesn't he?"

"That's a crime waiting to happen. The young mother has her purse beside her, but her attention is on the baby and the band. He's just waiting to make a move and she's going to lose her money and identification."

"How can you be so sure? Maybe he's just here for the music too."

"I arrested him more than once for just that very thing. He's a petty thief. Wait here, I'll be right back."

Laura watched as Patrick walked with purpose across the lawn and stood directly behind the young man. She could see them exchange words and suddenly the younger man left the area. As Patrick headed back to her side, he saw two people abandon the bench they were sitting on and waved her over. "This okay for you?" Patrick asked.

"Oh, it's great. What did you say to him?"

"I just reminded him of all the comforts of being in jail." Patrick's laughter made her join in with him.

"I can see how you were effective as a cop. Wait, is that an offensive term for you?"

"I've never been upset with being called a cop. I've certainly been called worse." The musicians announced they would be playing a last song and Laura found herself wishing the night wouldn't end. Reluctantly, she stood up.

"I guess we need to go." Most of the crowd was already standing, preparing for the last song and the end of the evening. Patrick joined her and together they walked down the sidewalk to their cars.

The breeze was picking up slightly as they reached her car. "I really enjoyed tonight. I feel a little funny, though." Laura looked up at him.

"I know what you mean. This will change our relationship, and that can be a bit scary."

"Scary good, right?" She seemed to need some confirmation from him, and Patrick didn't disappoint her. He bent down and they shared another kiss. "We'll be fine." He spoke as they ended their moment. "We've got all the time in the world to figure out where this is going."

"I like that. I'll call you in the morning and see what we can accomplish on the case." Opening her door, Laura smiled at him. "Thanks again."

"Drive safely. Why don't you text me when you get home."

Driving up the street, past the town square, Laura couldn't keep the smile from lighting up her face. It had been a surprise invitation, but she thoroughly enjoyed the time with Patrick. Her thoughts swirled in her head, but she refused to allow any negative vibes to spoil a perfectly good night.

Sitting in her car in the driveway, Laura sent a quick text to Patrick letting him know she was home safe and sound, then quickly went through the side door. "Vicky, I'm home."

Checking the time on her kitchen clock, Laura proceeded down the hall to the guest room and found it completely empty. Just as she was turning to leave, Laura noticed the note propped up on the dresser. Sensing danger, she quickly opened it and read:

"Sis, I'm happy that you've found someone to have fun with, you deserve it. I've been thinking long and hard about my life and I feel my only chance is with Randy. I'm taking a page from your book and throwing caution to the wind. Thank you for all your love and concern, but don't worry. I'll text you tomorrow. Be happy. I hope I can be, too."

Pulling her phone out of the pocket of her jeans, Laura quickly placed a call to Vicky. Not surprisingly, her sister didn't answer. Her next move was to send her a text. Once that was done, Laura placed a call to Patrick.

"Hey, pretty lady, what's up?"

"Vicky went back to Randy!"

His tone immediately changed, "Okay, don't panic. Calm down and tell me what she said."

"She left a note in the bedroom." Laura then read it to him.

"I assume you tried to call her."

"Yes, but she didn't answer, so I sent a text. She still hasn't answered me back. Patrick, I'm so scared. This is a huge mistake. She has no idea how dangerous that man is and what he's capable of!"

"Do you want me to come over there?" He maintained a calm, soothing voice.

Before answering, she hesitated a moment, gathering her thoughts. "No, no, I'll be fine. I'll just wait for Vicky to call me."

"Laura, you had to have known that this could happen. Vicky has been with Randy for a long time. You've done everything you could, but ultimately, it's her decision."

"I know, I know. Vicky has never been a strong person. I think that's why I feel so determined to help her."

"You're such a good sister. Just try to relax. I know that's not going to be an easy task. Laura, give her some time to figure things out. You've done everything you could."

"Sunny's calling. I'll call you tomorrow. Thank you, Patrick."

Switching calls, she heard Sunny's voice, "Nana, how are you doing? What's going on?"

Laura took a deep breath and tried to calm her nerves. "Hey, kiddo. How are you? What's going on?"

"I heard you and Patrick went out on a date. How'd that go?"

"Where did you hear that?"

"My dad talked with Auntie. What did you guys do? Was it fun?" Sunny's enthusiasm was hard to ignore.

Trying hard to tamp down her apprehension about Vicky's decision, Laura answered her granddaughter. "We met at Murphy's for dinner, then went to Courthouse Plaza to listen to a local band."

"Ooh, did you kiss? Was it good?" Sunny teased.

"Sunny! You are just too nosy for your own good." Laura admonished. "It was great!" She added and the two of them had a giggle together.

"Hey, little one, I have a favor to ask. You know what Patrick and I are working on, right?"

"Sure, Nana. What can I do?" Sunny was eager to help. "I will follow your instructions. I won't get into any trouble, I promise."

"That's good. I need you to text your Auntie. She's not answering me, so I just want to see if she'll get back to you. She went back to Randy, and I'm concerned. Don't alarm her, just see if you can get a response and then I won't worry." Laura hoped it sounded simple enough.

"I can do that! When I hear back from her, I'll let you know. Don't worry Nana, she'll be fine. Auntie is much stronger than you think."

"Love you, Sunshine!" Laura put her phone down and pondered her granddaughter's confidence in Vicky. Growing up with Vicky was fun but Laura remembered always having to rescue her sister from one problem or another. Once on the playground back in grade school, several girls accused Vicky of stealing a decorative pin from one of them. They were about to beat her up when Laura intervened, took Vicky to the bathroom and confronted her. Vicky opened her hand and showed her the pin in her fist. She'd held on to it so hard her hand was bleeding from being poked by the pin. Laura took the pin from her and together they went back out to the others. She remembered it as though it were yesterday. "My sister didn't steal your stupid pin! Let's look around and see if we can find it on the ground. It's got to be here somewhere."

The younger girls were so intimidated by her stance, they immediately spread out to look for it. Finally, one girl hollered as she picked up the brooch. "I found it!" With a smug look on her face, Laura scolded the others. "Next time, I hope you'll think twice before you accuse someone of stealing!" With that final comment, she took Vicky by the hand and they walked back into the school.

With tears streaming down her face, Vicky cried and apologized to her big sister. "I just wanted to look at it and it fell off. I wasn't stealing it, really!" Laura felt a smile cross her face as the memory subsided. Patrick was right, she had done everything she could for Vicky. It was time to let go.

Once in her room, Laura undressed and crawled into bed. Her phone was on the nightstand in case Vicky called, but her mind was on her date with Patrick. Being with him gave her a warm feeling, one she hadn't expected. He was smart, witty, and very considerate. It wouldn't be fair to compare him to Carl as the two of them were totally different men and she was in an entirely different state of mind now, but Laura suddenly realized that Patrick might be just the person she needed in her life.

Her thoughts were interrupted by the sound of a text on her phone. Laura read the short message from Sunny and let out a sigh. The text read, "Nana, Auntie got back to me and said she's doing fine. Hope this helps you relax."

Morning dawned and Laura reached for the remote to shut the blinds so she could catch a few more minutes of sleep. With each passing year, Laura found that sleep was a valuable commodity and she tried to get it whenever she could. The Gods of Sleep were against her, however, when she heard the text chime.

The message was from Josh, asking if she was up and once she responded, he called.

"Mom, did you hear from Vicky?"

"I didn't but Sunny did. Why? What's up?"

"Nothing really. I tried to reach her, but she didn't answer me either. How do you feel about her going back to Randy?" Josh asked.

Laura thought about her response, but finally answered her son, "She's been with him for over ten years now and I think Vicky is too afraid of being alone to make a permanent change."

"That's exactly what I'm thinking. As much as I love her, I've always wished she would be more confident and believe in herself. I feel Randy has always dominated her." Josh voiced his opinion.

"Oh, son, I agree but it's not up to us. You know we can't help who we fall in love with. You've heard the saying the heart wants what the heart wants, haven't you?"

His laughter betrayed his response, "Don't you think 'lust' has more to do with it than love?"

"Son, you're terrible! Your own divorce has tainted your opinions of life."

His laughter was contagious. "Mom, you're probably right, but I'm glad your divorce didn't stop you from your date last night. Did you have a good time?"

"Yes, I did. Working with Patrick has been enlightening, but we've not had much time to get to know each other on a personal level. He's a really nice guy."

"Yeah, I got that impression the day we worked on your deck. I was glad we got to do that. Well, got to go. Keep me in the loop. Love you, Mom."

"Love you too, son." Laura ended the call.

Laura wandered into the kitchen, getting the coffee ready and trying to decide if she wanted anything for breakfast. Plodding through the morning, Laura finally decided on toast and coffee. As she sat at the breakfast bar, she allowed her mind free reign and continued her thoughts about her sister's current circumstances.

Vicky was the instigator in this whole situation when she tried to convince Laura that Randy was guilty of killing his first wife. Those thoughts started this whole investigation. Maybe he didn't, she thought, trying to keep positive thoughts in her mind. All she wanted was for her sister to be safe and happy.

Finally deciding to get dressed, Laura went to her bedroom and as she was looking for her jeans and a top, her phone rang. Looking at the display, she saw that it was Patrick.

"Hey, what's going on?"

"I just wanted to see if you were alright last night after finding Vicky's note. You seemed a bit upset." His voice was soothing to her nerves.

"I'm fine. Thanks for asking. I'm still worried about Vicky, but I'm trying to let it go. I've been taking care of her for so long, it's hard."

"I completely understand that, but did you sleep well?" He asked.

"Actually, I did. After Sunny texted me, it put my mind at ease. Vicky responded to her text."

"Have you heard from her?" Patrick asked.

"Not personally. She seems to be avoiding me, but I understand that. That's why I asked Sunny to text her. I'm going to try again today."

"How are you doing, really?" He questioned Laura.

"I'm fine. I enjoyed our date. It was nice."

"I liked it, too. What do you have planned for today?"

"I'm going to putter around my house. It seems like forever since I cleaned and dusted, you know, all that housekeeping stuff." She laughed.

"I know that well, but I did finally hire someone to come in and do the little tasks twice a month."

"Oh, lucky you! I'm still plodding along on my own." She chuckled. "Thanks for last night. I really did enjoy it."

"We'll do it again. I should go. I need to give a bid on a new job. I'll talk to you later."

"That sounds great. Have fun."

"I'm not sure about having fun, but I'll give it my best. I'll talk to you later."

The rest of the day was spent doing the necessary housekeeping duties she had been neglecting. She'd texted her sister right after talking with Patrick, but still hadn't heard back from her. Working hard to ignore the nagging feelings of impending doom, Laura devoted herself to the cleaning tasks.

She was mopping the guest bathroom when she heard a familiar voice. "Nana! Where are you?"

"Sweetie, I'm back here."

"Oh, you're working so hard!" Sunny had a huge grin on her face.

"You can help me if you want." Laura challenged her.

"Ah, no. I'm good, but you're doing a great job."

"You're such a good cheerleader, little one." They hugged. "Go get us something cool to drink. I'll be right out."

As she got to the kitchen, Laura saw that Sunny had poured cold iced tea for them. At the breakfast bar, she sat on the stool and sipped the wonderfully refreshing drink. "Thanks. I've been working hard today."

"I can see that. Have you heard from Auntie?"

"I'm not sure. I haven't checked." She reached for her phone. "Yeah, she finally answered my text."

"What's going on?" Sunny asked.

"She didn't say much, that she was going to the mall."

"That's all? That's kinda weird." Sunny spoke her opinion.

"Why do you think that?"

"Earlier, she texted me that she and Randy were going to have a day to themselves. They were going to try and work things out. Why would she go to the mall?"

Ignoring the suspicions raised by Sunny's comments, Laura pretended nonchalance. "Maybe they're going together. Maybe he's going to buy her something expensive. You know how Vicky likes new things and besides, he may be trying to apologize."

"Yeah, you're probably right. Well, Nana, got to go. Love you." With those words and a kiss on the cheek, Sunny left.

The void in the room was filled with tension and worry. The nagging feeling of trouble ahead wouldn't leave her alone. Reaching for her phone, she started to call Patrick but stopped herself. I need to handle this on my own, she thought, but a quick knock at the kitchen door got her attention.

Before she could answer, the door opened and the man in her thoughts appeared. Patrick said, "Hey! I thought you said you were going to work today. This doesn't look anything like I imagined."

Without hesitation, she hugged him tightly. "I'm glad you're here."

"Has something happened?" He held her tenderly.

"No, well, I don't know. I haven't heard anything. I just can't seem to get rid of these dark clouds today. I wish Vicky had just stayed here."

"Let's go outside. Sometimes, when I can't get rid of dark thoughts invading my brain, I try to get outdoors and let the beauty of nature help me."

"I think I'm ready for some alcohol. How about you?" She asked.

"Sure, just pour me some of what you're having."

Finally sitting on the new deck, Laura and Patrick inhaled the fresh mountain air and enjoyed the silence of the evening hours. She'd poured them a generous portion of wine and as she took a sip, Laura said, "I'm glad you're here. I've been trying since last night to let Vicky go, but it's near to impossible. I'm angry because she's the one who started this whole thing. What if Randy didn't kill his first wife? What if he's just a jerk? What if we're the ones on the wrong trail?"

Eleven

Laura opened her eyes slowly at first. She looked around to make sure she was in her own bedroom and alone. She was. Lying back on her pillow with her head pounding in pain, Laura closed her eyes and tried valiantly to remember the events of the night before. Climbing out of bed, Laura realized that she was still in her jeans and T-shirt.

She and Patrick had shared at least two bottles of wine and sat on the deck well into the night. Flashes of memory popped into her throbbing head as she remembered Patrick keeping up with her, glass for glass. Normally a conservative drinker, Laura had indulged her apprehension about her sister and ignored her own good sense.

Self-pity was never a part of her life, so Laura finally made the effort to get herself out of her bed. Once in the bathroom, she splashed cold water on her face and tried to straighten her hair, which was in total disarray. Finally making her way down the hall, she was shocked to see Patrick in the guest bedroom. He had removed his boots and belt but lay there on his stomach in his shirt and jeans. A slight smile crossed her face as she tiptoed past the room to make the coffee.

She checked her phone for messages but saw none. With the coffee done, Laura poured herself a cup but with a second thought, poured another for Patrick. She saw he had rolled over and as she waved the hot cup near his face, Patrick opened his eyes. "Wow, that smells good." He sat up and reached for the hot brew. "Lady, you put on a good party last night."

She sat down on the edge of the bed. "Sorry about that. You didn't have to keep up with me." Her grin told him she was teasing.

"I couldn't let you suffer alone, could I?" He sipped slowly. "How are you doing today?"

"Other than a pounding headache, I'm fine. By the way, how did I get in my bed?"

"Well, you needed just a little help, but you'll notice you still had your clothes on." The gleam in his eyes made her smile.

"I'm glad you stayed and didn't drive with all that wine in you." She enjoyed this light banter between them.

"Have you heard from Vicky?" He asked and watched the look of dismay cross her pretty features.

"Not yet, but I'm going to call her later and if she won't answer me, I'll hunt her down and make her talk to me. I'm not mad, just worried."

He leaned over and kissed her on the cheek. "She knows that. She's got to be churning through a lot of emotions right now. You two will straighten it out."

"Thanks." She stood up. "Now, how about some breakfast? I don't remember eating anything last night and I'm hungry."

"Sounds good. I'll be right in to help you."

Her phone pinged just as she stepped into the kitchen. Seeing the name on the screen stopped her in her tracks. She looked up as Patrick walked in and held it up. "It's a text from Randy. What the hell does he want?"

"There's only one way to find out."

"I'm scared, you look at it." She unlocked her screen and handed it to him.

From the look on his face, Laura knew it wasn't good news. Quickly grabbing the phone from him, she read the text. "What does this mean? Why does he think Vicky is here?"

When Patrick didn't answer, she saw he was on his own phone. He wasn't talking much; the conversation was all on the other end. "Well, let me know if you hear anything. Thanks."

"That was Nick, my connection with the sheriff's office. I just wanted to see if they knew anything. So far, they haven't heard from Vicky or Randy."

"Well, I'm going to call that bastard! I'll find out what kind of a game he's playing."

"Wait! Laura, think about this. We can't let him know that we're onto him. Try to contact Vicky and see where she's staying. We have to play this cool, or he might panic and really cause some big trouble."

Deep in thought, Laura sat at the breakfast bar and stared at her phone. "This detective work isn't so easy, especially when you're personally involved. Is it?"

He sat next to her and reached for her hand. "It's never easy, no matter what. What's important for us right now is to not tip our hand. We need Randy to think we're playing the game his way. Text him back and tell him that you haven't heard from Vicky and ask him what happened."

She did as she was told, and they waited. "I can't stand this!"

Laura visibly jumped when the phone rang. "It's him! What do I say?"

"Just let him do most of the talking. Don't let on that we know anything about his past. Just be concerned with Vicky and her problems. Put it on speaker so I can hear what he has to say."

"Hey, Randy, what's going on?" She tried to sound calm.

"Can I talk with her?" His manner was gruff and arrogant.

"I told you she's not here. She left me a note and said she was going home. What happened? I thought you two were going to try and work things out."

He hesitated before answering. "Everything was fine the first night she came home but then yesterday she wanted to go shopping. I didn't. She got mad and left in a huff. I just assumed she ran to big sister again."

It sounded rehearsed. Laura looked at Patrick and shook her head. "Well, I haven't heard. I've been trying to reach her, but she hasn't returned my calls."

"I think I need to call the police."

She looked to see that Patrick was shaking his head in agreement.

"I think that's a good idea. I'm the only one that Vicky would come to and if she's missing, we need to get some official help. Let me know what they say."

"Yeah, and you let me know if she shows up at your place." With that, Randy ended the call.

"Oh, my God! Patrick, what has he done?" She envisioned the worst.

"Look, I know this is not going to be a very good day in your life, but I need you to try and remain calm." He stood up.

"Where are you going?"

"I'm going downtown. Do you want to go with me?"

"You bet!" She rushed to put on clean clothes and comb her hair as fast as she could. "Let's go."

The short trip to the sheriff's office was made in quick time. As they walked into the building, Patrick turned and spoke. "Let me do the talking. We'll get more information if they think you're just a concerned sister. Okay?"

Soon, they were let in behind a locked door and as they rounded the corner, an older man greeted them. "Patrick! Good to see you, son. How can I help?"

After they entered the man's office, Patrick made introductions. Laura shook his hand. "Nice to meet you, Nick."

The two men talked as Patrick brought Nick up to date on the disappearance of her sister but left out the part that they suspected Randy of killing his first wife. Nick turned to Laura, "She hasn't gotten in contact with you at all?"

"No, not me, but she did answer my granddaughter's text the day after she went back home. I think she's feeling somewhat embarrassed. Vicky has always been a little impulsive. She likes having attention, too."

"What do you think has happened?"

She looked at Patrick before answering. "I think my sister has trouble in her marriage and is trying to save it at any cost."

"Would she disappear just to make her husband sweat?" The older detective asked.

"No, I don't think she would do that." Laura tried to answer honestly. She noticed Nick was taking notes the entire time. "You have to understand, Vicky has been spoiled most of her life and Randy contributed to that after they were married. She just wants to have a happy marriage and live a good life."

Patrick finally spoke up. "Nick, we just want you to keep us in the loop if anything comes up. Laura is concerned about her sister and wants her back home, safe and sound." He stood.

Laura made one last appeal to the detective. "My sister is a wonderful woman and all I want is for her to be safe. Any help you can give us is greatly appreciated."

"I'll do what I can, Laura, and we'll keep in touch with you."

She reached for Patrick's hand and held it as they walked to his truck. He opened the door for her. Neither one spoke.

Driving slowly through the busy downtown traffic, Laura finally said what was on her mind.

"Patrick, I think we're facing a horrible ending to this. Vicky has no place to go. I can't imagine her going to a hotel and she doesn't really have any close friends to stay with."

"Let's just take it one moment at a time. Nick will let us know if and when anything is found. Are you hungry? Would you like to stop anywhere?"

"I just want to go home, so I can keep busy working there and try to wait patiently for some answers."

"I have some work to do for a customer. It's just a small job but I'll keep my phone handy."

As they pulled into her driveway, Laura started to open her door before he could. "Patrick, I can't thank you enough for everything you've done."

"That sounds like a goodbye."

"Not at all! We are in this until the end, Mister!" He was by her side, and she leaned into his strong body. "I'm going to look forward to a second date." Their kiss was strong and passionate.

"I'll call you later or sooner, if I hear something." He gave her a quick kiss before getting back into his truck and pulling away.

She placed one more call to Vicky. "Sis, please, please call me. I'm worried. We can work it all out together."

As she stepped into the kitchen, she had a second thought and called her son. "Josh! How's it going?"

"I'm good, Mom. In fact, I'm great. I just got a call and I'm starting my new job next week."

"Oh, honey, that's great. I'm thrilled for you."

"What's up with you?" Josh asked.

"Well, I'm in a bit of a tizzy. Vicky went back home to Randy two days ago and she's now missing." Her voice cracked as she had a sudden realization of how bad the situation had become.

"Mom, what can I do? I haven't talked with her for a couple of days. Are you sure she's missing?"

"Yes. Randy called and told me he's going to report her as missing to the police. I'm beside myself with worry. I feel so helpless." She allowed a few tears to fall down her cheeks.

"Do you want me to come over?" Her son offered.

"No, I know you have things to do. I just wanted to let you know and see if you've heard from her. If she contacts you, call me right away!"

"I definitely will. She'll be fine, you'll see." Josh tried to console his mother.

Looking around the room, Laura finally started cleaning the kitchen. She scrubbed, swept and dusted every corner. Checking her phone, she saw that there were no messages from Vicky or Patrick. The clock on the wall said it was time for lunch and her growling stomach agreed.

Her phone buzzed and the nerves in her stomach tightened as she saw it was Patrick. "What?" She skipped any formalities.

"I just heard from Nick. Randy did file a missing person's report. He also let me know that he recognized Randy's last name. With the new missing person's report in the system, it brought up Donna's disappearance. He now has the file on the first wife."

"That could be good, right?"

"In fact, he said that put Vicky's missing person report on top priority. He sent officers out looking for her car at the mall parking lot." Patrick laid out the facts like the trained professional that he was. "Laura?"

"I'm glad that you let me know. I'm trying to remain calm, but my mind keeps wanting to go to dark places." It was getting more and more difficult to keep her emotions in check.

"I'll be over as soon as I finish this job."

"Thank you but do what you have to do, Patrick. I'll be fine." Her words were meant to reassure but fell short.

As she signed off, Laura cleared her lunch dish, headed down the hallway to her office and sat down at her computer to study the pictures of her notes that had been written on the walls. While reviewing her notes about the disappearance of Randy's first wife, Laura tried to find any clue that might have been overlooked by the original team of detectives. She also reviewed the video interview she and Patrick had done with Randy and Donna's daughter, Lisa.

Reviewing the recording, although she couldn't put her finger on it, Laura felt something was awry with Lisa's responses. She turned the sound off and simply observed Lisa's movements and facial expressions. Quickly pausing the recording, Laura noticed that Lisa seemed to be looking not at the screen but beyond it. She reversed the video for several seconds and replayed that particular scene.

Laura was now convinced that someone else was in the room with Lisa during their conversation.

"Nana! Where are you?" Sunny's voice came from the front room.

"I'm in the office. Come on back, Sweetie." Laura welcomed the interruption.

Sunny came into the room with a warm smile and a hug for her grandmother. "How are you doing?" She glanced at the computer screen. "What are you doing?"

"I'm trying to solve a sixteen-year-old crime. I was hoping I could find something that would help me determine if Randy is the bad guy we think he is."

"Any luck?" Sunny sat on the corner of the big desk.

"Maybe you can help me. Here is part of the interview Patrick and I conducted with Randy and Donna's daughter, Lisa. The sound is muted so just concentrate on her actions. Let me know your impression of her behavior as she answers our questions."

They both watched and rewatched the section that Laura was puzzled over. "Play it one more time, Nana."

"Well, what do you think?"

"I think she was being coached by someone across from her in the room. What did you think?" Sunny waited for an answer.

"I think you are spot on! You're very good as an amateur detective."

"You're the best, Nana. Have you heard anything from Aunt Vicky?"

Laura explained the latest developments. Sunny hugged her tightly. "Oh, it doesn't look good, does it?"

"Keep praying. Don't give up hope, okay?" Laura soothed her.

"I have to get to class. Are you going to be alright? Is Patrick coming over?" As they walked to the kitchen door, they hugged one more time.

"Yes, he said he would come over later. I'm going to clean out that closet in the guest room. That will keep me busy for a while."

"Love you, Nana." Sunny waved goodbye as she pulled out of the driveway.

With a huge sigh, Laura found herself pulling all the boxes and clothing out of that closet, stacking everything on the bed and started going through it. Separating everything into piles, she kept thoughts of Vicky out of her mind. After an hour or so, she started putting the items to keep back into the closet. Standing back, Laura was pleased with her efforts.

"Now, what do I do with you?" She spoke to the pile of clothes and boxes that she no longer wanted and Laura took everything to the front room. She'd made up her mind that the local veteran's thrift store could benefit from her work.

Needing some fresh air, she stepped out onto the deck and sat on a lawn chair. The sky was covered with clouds, blocking out the sunshine. A slight breeze was blowing, and she could hear the neighbor's dogs barking. She had her phone in her back pocket and the buzzing disturbed the peaceful moment.

"Hello."

"Laura, this is Nick."

Immediately all of her senses were on full alert. "Did you find Vicky?" She was afraid of his answer.

"No, we haven't, but some of her identification and credit cards were found. We've intensified our search in that area of town."

Laura put her phone down for a few seconds. "Nick, where was this found?" She knew he was hesitant to tell her. "I just need to know, maybe I can help search for her."

"I know you want to help, but you need to leave this to the professionals. I just wanted to give you an update."

"I know you're the expert, but I can't just sit here doing nothing! Did you call Patrick?"

"Yes, he suggested I call you directly. Laura, we're doing everything we can to find her. I'll keep you updated." The phone went dead.

Laura immediately called Patrick, who answered right away.

"Yes?"

"Did Nick tell you where they found her ID?" Her voice shook with fear, but the demand for information was clear in her request. She realized Patrick was aware she would be calling.

"No, he didn't. Please give him time to search the area. He'll let us know what he finds. I can only imagine how hard this is on you. I'm asking you to trust me, trust Nick. Please." Patrick waited for her to respond.

"Patrick, you should know by now that I'm not one to sit on the sidelines and do nothing. You and I both know that Randy is responsible for this. Oh my God! I don't want to lose my sister." Her pain was palpable.

His voice was soft as he tried to console her. "Laura, please, please, give Nick time to investigate. I'll be finished here in just a few minutes, and I'll come over. Stay where you are. Laura?"

"I can't give you my word that I'll stay here, but I can tell you that I'll make smart decisions about my actions. This is the best I can give you."

"I guess that I have to accept that. I'll be there as fast as I can."

"Thanks for being her for me, Patrick." She ended the call.

As she was changing her clothes, Laura heard Sunny calling from the kitchen. "Nana! Where are you?"

As Sunny came into her room, she looked up. "Hey, kiddo, what are you doing here?"

Sunny stumbled on her words before answering, "I'm in between classes and thought I would see how you're doing."

"You were never a good liar, little one!"

"Nana! Why would you say that?"

"Did Patrick call you?"

Sunny looked at her grandmother but couldn't continue without a confession. "Nana, he's only concerned about you. Please, let me stay here with you until he gets here."

"I can't believe it!" Laura finished dressing. "What the hell! Who is he to decide what's best for me!" She continued her rant.

Sunny sat on the edge of the bed and waited for her grandmother to finish expressing her frustrations. Finally, Laura turned to face her. "Sunny, I love you and appreciate what you and Patrick are trying to do, but I just can't sit here and do nothing while Vicky is missing! The worst part of it all, is that I think Randy has played a role in her disappearance and God help him if my sister comes to any harm!" Unable to hold back her tears any longer, Laura sat down beside Sunny and allowed her fears to culminate in a tirade of pain.

Soon both were in the midst of a crying jag as they held on to each other. Realizing that Patrick was now standing in the doorway of her bedroom, Laura tried to stop the flow of tears. The look of care and concern on his handsome face was alarming.

"What?" She asked.

"You need to come with me."

"Oh, my God! They found her, didn't they?"

"Laura, please, let's go." He held his hand out.

"Nana, I'm going with you." Sunny stood up.

Patrick started to protest, but Laura stopped him. "We need to finish this together."

"You have to know that this isn't going to be pretty. If it is Vicky, there's an active crime scene and we don't know what the actual situation is with her until we get there.

"Patrick, I know that you are so much more experienced about these things than we are, but I want to be there for Nana and for my Auntie." Sunny's lips trembled as she spoke, but determination showed on her face.

The late afternoon weather was threatening to change as dark clouds started rolling into the city. Once in Patrick's truck, there was little conversation between the three of them. Finally, Laura asked, "Where was she found? I always thought Prescott was a safe place to live. I've not found any bad neighborhoods, really." She found herself rambling.

"Nana, I'm scared." Sunny's voice came from the back seat.

"Oh, Sweetie, so am I."

"Laura, I want you to understand that Nick is letting us in on this as a favor to me."

"I do understand and appreciate it, Patrick. Has Randy been called?"

"Not yet. Nick wants to process the entire crime scene thoroughly before notifying Randy." She felt Patrick looking at her and Laura met his look. "You won't have to deal with him for now."

Patrick turned onto Smoke Tree Lane. This entire area had expensive custom-built homes on both sides of the street. "We're heading to the golf course at Prescott Lakes, aren't we?"

"You know this area?"

"Vicky always wanted to live here. She loved the big homes and the thought of being a part of the country club really appealed to her."

As they approached the entrance to the golf course maintenance yard, she noticed many official vehicles with lots of people working in the crime area. A crack of thunder startled Laura. She looked to the heavens and then back to the scene before them. She saw several canopies surrounded by screens protecting the workers from being observed as they performed their forensic tasks. Patrick slowed down to talk with the officer just in front of the crime scene tape. "Hey, Nick is expecting us."

The officer lifted the tape so they could get the truck into the parking lot and pointed to a spot where they should park. Laura was taking it all in but as soon as she saw Vicky's car, she felt a huge lump in her throat. "Oh, my God! That's her car! Patrick, I don't know if I can do this."

"Nana, you have to do it for Auntie. She would want you by her side." Sunny's timid voice was close, and Laura felt her granddaughter's hand on her arm. "I'll stay here and wait for you guys."

"I'll be right back. Wait here until I talk with Nick." Patrick got out and they watched as he approached his friend. He turned and waved at Laura. Reluctantly, she got out of the truck and walked over to the two men.

"That's her car." She spoke to Nick, although her glance never left Vicky's car. "Is she in it?" When Nick didn't answer, Laura finally looked at the older detective. "Where is she?" She felt Patrick edge closer to her.

Nick looked at Patrick before answering. With a shake of his head, Nick took a deep breath. "She was in the trunk."

"Oh, my God! Oh, my God!" Laura reached for Patrick. "What happened to her?"

"Let's go over here and you can sit down." Nick ushered them to one of the canopies where they found some folding chairs to sit on. "Are you sure you want all the details?"

"Give it to me straight. If she went through hell, I want to know what he did to her."

"Laura, I don't think your sister knew what was coming and in all my years of investigation work, I can honestly say she died quickly from the first blow." Over Laura's bowed head, Nick locked eyes with Patrick. Without saying a word, the two men agreed that she needed to hear all the gruesome facts.

"Someone hit her so hard on the back of the head that she died instantly. When we found her in the trunk, she had a bungee cord wrapped around her neck, but she was already dead, so it was unnecessary violence."

"That shows that whoever did this had a lot of anger towards Vicky, didn't they?" Tears were brimming in her eyes, and she gratefully took the tissue handed her. Light raindrops started falling outside the canopy, matching her sadness.

"Yes, it appears to be overkill."

"Then it was personal and not just a random robbery or something like that?"

"No, it wasn't just an unplanned act of violence. Whoever did this intended for Vicky to suffer. To answer your question, it was a very personal act of savagery." With all his years of experience, Nick hated telling the family the cruel details.

"Hey, Nick, you need to take this call." Another officer came up and handed the phone to Nick.

Nick stepped away, Patrick took the opportunity to speak quietly to Laura. "Are you okay?"

"No, I'm not!" She stopped herself before saying more that she would regret. "Patrick, my sister is dead, and we both know that Randy did this! How in the world could I possibly be okay?"

Before Patrick could answer, Nick came closer. "That was her husband. He's on his way here."

"I want to see my sister before he gets here." Laura was defiant.

"Laura, I don't think that's wise." Patrick immediately replied and Nick confirmed.

"You won't see the sister you knew. She's been through a horrible attack, and it isn't a pretty sight." Nick added.

"I've seen her at her worst and she needs me now more than ever. I insist that you allow me to see her!"

With a sigh of resignation, Nick finally agreed. "Come with me, but I must warn you, we just took her out of the trunk of the car. The body won't be processed until we get her to the coroner's office. Laura, I beg you, wait, please!"

Standing strong, she firmly spoke, "My sister needs me, and I've always been there for her. I've taken care of Vicky for a very long time. I need to be there for her now."

Twelve

"Laura, won't you reconsider?" Patrick tried one more time. Seeing the look of determination on her face, he took her arm and escorted her to the canopy a few feet away. There, she saw a team of people standing by her sister's body on a gurney. As they approached, one attendant looked at Nick for instructions.

"It's okay." He spoke. "We need a positive ID."

With great trepidation, Laura came closer. She felt her heart pounding in her chest as she waited for the technician to remove the sheet that covered her sister's face. She let out a groan from the depths of her being as she saw Vicky lying there. She turned away for a moment to regain her composure. Laura took a deep breath, turning around slowly allowing herself more time to comprehend the amount of damage done to the body of her beloved sister.

She reached out and touched her lightly. There was no warmth, no life left in her sister's body. Tasting the salty tears that were now flowing down her face, she spoke tenderly, "Oh, my beautiful sister. What has he done to you? I promise you he will pay." Pausing for just a minute, she continued, "Be in peace, Little Sis. I love you."

Turning, Laura melted into Patrick's waiting embrace. He guided her slowly away from the tent towards his truck as she held her head down and cried freely. "This should have never happened. We should have been able to stop him!" Her anger was mounting when she felt Patrick stop suddenly. She looked up and saw Randy standing in their path.

Quietly, Patrick whispered to her, "Don't do anything foolish, Laura. We will uncover the evidence to prove he did this."

Suddenly she saw Sunny approaching behind Randy. As soon as she saw her grandmother, Sunny ran into her open arms. "Nana, I saw him pulling up, I wanted to warn you, but he got ahead of me."

"It's okay." Laura's voice was thick with emotion. Turning to Patrick, "Please take her back to the truck. I'll be right there."

He hesitated, but she reassured Patrick. "I need to do this my way. I can't let it go and not say something to him." Randy was still just standing there, watching them.

She waited until she thought Patrick and Sunny were out of earshot. As she approached Randy, it was all she could do to contain her rage. With whispered tones, she spoke, "You think I don't know what you've done. My sister has suffered, and you have her blood on your hands. I won't rest until you have felt one tenth of the pain Vicky did!" She didn't wait for him to respond, but just walked away. She heard him call after her, "I now know why they called you El Diablo Roja! You are a devil."

The truck was running as Patrick and Sunny waited for Laura. She got in and they sped away, heading back to her home. In the kitchen, Laura pulled out the wine and offered some to Patrick. He declined. She poured a generous glass for herself.

"Nana, it was Auntie, wasn't it?" Sunny's voice sounded much younger than her seventeen years. "I don't think I've known anyone who died."

Giving her a big hug, Laura tried to comfort Sunny. "At times like this, people try to say things to make you feel better, but, Sweetie, nothing I can say will do that. We'll just have to muddle our way through this moment by moment."

"What did you say to Randy?" Patrick asked.

"I told him that Vicky had suffered and I promised him that he'll feel all the pain she did and then some. He's not a stupid person and I couldn't pretend that I didn't know what he's capable of doing. I didn't say anything about his first wife, nor the fact that we know he's committing robbery." She looked directly at Patrick.

"He called you a name as you left. What was that?"

"You heard that?" She was surprised. "Back in the day, I worked at a manufacturing shop with a crew of men, and they gave me a nickname, El Diablo Roja which means Red Devil. They constantly made fun of my red hair. I had to be tougher than any of the men and they didn't like it. Vicky used to tease me with that name when I made her mad."

"What do we do now, Nana?"

"We make funeral arrangements for her."

"Won't that be up to Uncle Randy?" she asked innocently.

"Under normal circumstances, the husband would be the one to do that, but because Randy's under suspicion of murder, I don't think he'll be involved." Patrick answered.

"Did Nick tell you that?" Laura asked.

"Not in so many words but combined with the evidence on his first wife's death and the fact that DNA technology has advanced so much since then, they'll have no trouble placing him at the crime scene."

"He's going to be a man on the run, don't you think?" Laura took another drink of her wine and then added, "I wouldn't want him to get away."

Sunny was sitting close to her grandmother. Laura sensed her need for comfort and put her arm around the young girl. "Baby, this is a horrible thing for you to have to deal with and for that, I'm sorry."

"I think we should call my dad. Nana, would you do that?"

"Sure." With that Laura placed a call to her son. "Josh…" Her voice broke, but she found the strength to move on. "They found Vicky." The rest of the conversation went quickly.

"Your dad's on his way over here. I think we need to fix something to eat." Laura stated.

"I couldn't possibly eat anything, Nana, but I'll help you. I think I need to keep active. If I sit still, I'll just go crazy with all the thoughts flying around in my head." Sunny was crying again.

"I think I'll go back and see what Nick has found. Maybe I can help." Patrick stood up, grabbed his hat and headed to the kitchen door when Laura stopped him.

"I can't thank you enough." She reached up to kiss his cheek. Patrick turned to her, and their lips met in a tender kiss meant to soothe and comfort.

"You and your family need some time together. I'll call you later." He ran his hand down her cheek and wiped her tears.

"Nana, how are we going to live without her?" Sunny could barely get the words out.

"I don't know, I just don't know. I should've done more to keep her safe."

"Please, Nana, you can't beat yourself up. We all worked very hard to help her. Auntie did have a mind of her own and always did what she wanted." Sunny tried to console her grandmother.

They were working on putting some food together, even though both didn't feel they could eat at all, when Josh came through the kitchen door and immediately pulled both into a big hug. "What happened? Where was she found?"

As they sat at the kitchen table, Laura tried to control her emotions and explain the situation in full. "There's more to this than you know. A couple of weeks ago, Vicky called me in a panic. We met at Charley's and she told me that she thought Randy had killed his first wife."

"You've got to be kidding! Why would she think that?"

Laura spilled told the whole story including Sunny's involvement. Josh raised his hand to stop her. "You mean my daughter has been involved in a murder investigation and no one thought to tell me?" His anger was evident.

"Daddy, I was never in any danger. Nana and Patrick wouldn't allow that. I just did a little spying for them."

Trying to understand their reasoning and calming down, Josh said, "Go on. Tell me the rest."

"We found out that Randy is involved in big-time theft. That's how he is able to live in that big house and has more money than he actually earns. I think Vicky found out about his crimes and that's why she's dead." Laura cried. Reaching over and placing his hand on hers, Josh encouraged his mother. "Mom, tell me the rest."

"She was found in the trunk of her car. She'd been hit on the back of her head, blunt force trauma, they called it. There was a bungee cord around her neck but Nick, he's the detective, said she was probably dead from the blow to the head." Between tears and gulps for air, Laura finally spoke. "They let me see her. Oh, Son, I should have stopped her from going back to him. I can't believe she's gone."

"Mom, I'm sure you did everything you could for her. Where was her car found?" Josh tried to get all the information he could.

"That's the weird part of this. Her car was located in a great neighborhood, just over in the Prescott Country Club area. It may seem naïve of me, but you just don't think of murder happening in a nice place."

"So, what happens now?" He asked.

"Well, we need to plan her funeral, for one thing. I intend to have a serious conversation with Nick and see where they are in arresting Randy for this!" Laura stood up. "I can't just sit here and do nothing."

"You need to stay here. Patrick might come back with some good news, like they've already got him." Sunny reasoned, as she started putting plates on the table. "Let's eat these tacos."

Without conversation, each forced themselves to try and eat the meal. Finally, Laura got up and started cleaning the dishes. "I think I need to be alone. You two go on home." She shook her head as her son started to speak. "I will stay right here. I'm going to go over all the information we've collected. I want to be able to hand some solid evidence over to Nick."

"I don't think you should be alone." Josh stated.

"Look, I'm a big girl and I'll be fine. Besides, Patrick said he'd call me later. Go, please." She pressed them to agree. Very reluctantly, they left her with a promise to check in on her later.

Turning the light on in her office, Laura stared at the computer screen saver. It was a picture of the last Thanksgiving family gathering. She loved to cook for others and her family always enjoyed the meals she prepared. In the photo everyone was laughing and sitting around the fully-laden table. More tears fell as reality settled heavily on her heart. She touched her sister's picture on the computer screen. Vicky was gone. As anger surged through her veins, Laura thought, the best way I can vindicate her senseless death is to prove that Randy killed her. With that thought on her mind, Laura started poring through her notes again. She began organizing the interviews and notes according to the people involved.

Realizing she needed a larger space, Laura found the folding table in the bedroom closet and set it up in the office along the wall. Each pile started growing as she sorted the papers and pictures onto the table. Carefully reviewing each piece of evidence, one thing jumped out at her.

She read through the notes she made after her visit with her former neighbor Trisha, who had told Laura about Randy doing home improvement projects just after his first wife disappeared. Maybe he's like me, she thought to herself, he needs to stay busy when stressed. She stared at her own notes again. Trisha's husband helped him move some old furniture out of the garage, but he also helped pour a new backyard patio.

A noise from the kitchen alerted her that she wasn't alone. Cautiously she moved down the hallway and was immediately relieved when she heard Patrick's voice. "Wow! You scared me!" She told him.

"I can see that." He pointed to her gun. "Where is everyone? I thought they would stay with you."

"I wanted to be alone. I have to process everything that's happened. I've always visualized my life as sorting mail, putting envelopes into slots as they come down the conveyor belt. Every now and then you get a Christmas rush, and you're overwhelmed trying to sort everything into the correct bin. That's what I have to do with Vicky's death. Find the proper place for it in my life."

"I can understand that. This is something no one should ever have to deal with in their lifetime." Patrick moved closer to her.

She took him by the hand. "Come into the office. I want to show you what I've done." His hand was warm and comforting. Laura was reluctant to let it go but when they stepped into the room, Patrick left her side to look over the stacks on the table.

"This is good. You've organized things well. What conclusions have you come up with?" He perched on the side of her desk.

Sitting down at her computer, Laura pulled up the video of the interview with Randy's daughter. "Watch this without the sound and tell me what you think."

With more patience than she thought he had, Patrick asked her to play it again before responding. "I think she was being coached. I think there was someone in the room with her."

"That's exactly what Sunny and I thought!"

"What else do you have?"

"Remember when you and I talked about Randy pouring a new patio right after Donna disappeared? Is there a way of finding something underneath it without digging up the concrete?"

"Yes, there is GPR." When he saw the look of confusion on Laura's face, Patrick expanded, "It's called Ground Penetrating Radar, which can detect anomalies underground. The technology has been used for years to find unmarked graves."

"What would it take to do that on the patio at Randy's old house?"

"We could ask the owners but if they refuse, it will take a court order. That would require some sort of proof, not just the memories of a former neighbor."

"We keep coming up against roadblocks. You know Randy did it and I know he did it and now he's killed Vicky! Oh, my God, Patrick, he's going to get away with another murder." She held her head down and allowed tears to fall again.

Patrick pulled her up from the chair and into his arms. "You've got to get out of this office. Laura, trust that Nick and the other officers are doing their best to collect all the DNA and evidence possible. I think Nick is convinced that Randy did this and he's a good enough detective to get an arrest."

"I feel so angry! I should never have left her alone. If I'd only…"

He stopped her. "You can't do this to yourself. Believe me, I've got enough guilt for the two of us."

As his confession dawned on her, Laura looked up into his eyes and saw the demons that were haunting Patrick. "I'm so sorry. I didn't realize how deeply this has affected you too. Oh, Patrick, what are we going to do?"

"Right now, we're going to go out back and sit on that new deck of yours and just enjoy the evening. Come on." Taking her by the hand, they stopped long enough to gather a bottle of wine and two glasses and then stepped out into the darkness to savor the beautiful spring evening weather.

Time passed by quietly. They sat side by side in the lounge chairs without speaking. Heavy thoughts clouded their minds. Finally, Laura broke the silence, "Patrick, I know that both of us are feeling horrible, but if I was honest with myself, I don't think that we could have stopped this from happening. Let's just move forward with our evidence and help Nick arrest Randy."

"I'm glad you feel that way. Conducting an investigation can cripple you. I know it's very personal right now, but we'll get through this." Reaching over, he put his hand over hers.

As they got up, Laura surprised him, "Would you stay the night?"

His answer was slow in coming. "I will, but in your spare room. Is that okay?"

"I think that's perfect. I just want you in the house, close by."

As they stopped in the hall by the guest bedroom, Laura looked up in time to receive his kiss. She responded but ended it quickly and headed down to her bedroom. Shutting her door, she leaned against the cool, wooden surface and tasted more salty tears sliding down her face. Tossing and turning for most of the night, Laura finally got up and wandered down the hall. She stopped at the open door and stared at Patrick lying there.

As she started to move away, she heard him speak. "Laura, what is it?"

She slowly moved to the side of the bed and sat on the edge. "I didn't get to say goodbye."

Patrick sat up and hugged her to him. "My sweet lady, I'm so sorry. I wish I could take your pain away."

"Just hold me." She moved beside the shirtless man as he laid back down, holding her in his arms. It had been a long time since she was next to a man in bed, but this was as far from a romantic situation as it could be. Laura felt his warmth and comfort through the covers and was grateful that he was there.

His phone ringing brought her abruptly awake as Patrick shifted away to take the call. Laura sat up and started to leave the room, when he motioned for her to wait. She listened to his answers.

"Yes, Nick, we'll be there. Thanks for the call."

"What's happening? Did they arrest him?" She was hopeful but the look on Patrick's face dashed those hopes.

He was sitting up, but the sheet was still covering his lower body. "Get dressed. We need to go see Nick."

Without hesitation, Laura hurried to her room and pulled on her jeans and a top, ran a comb through her unruly hair and brushed her teeth. As she went down the hall, she saw that Patrick was dressed and waiting for her.

"Patrick, what did Nick say?"

"It's not good."

"Tell me!" she demanded. "I can take it."

"Randy is missing. He was cooperating, but his lawyer told him that he was the number one suspect. He's lawyered up and now they don't know where he went."

"Oh, my God! Can it get any worse? I knew I should have gone to his house to watch him!"

Patrick led the way out of her house to his truck. He drove quickly and in just a few minutes they were downtown at the sheriff's office. Once in front of Nick's desk, Laura released her frustrations, "How the hell could you let this happen? He's guilty. You know it and we know it. Why wasn't he being watched?"

"Look, I know this isn't the news you wanted to hear." Nick raised his hand to stop her response. "I can't imagine what you're going through, but you need to listen to me. He was already gone when my officer got to the house. The last conversation I had with Randy was when he told me to talk to his lawyer. Immediately I sent a team out, but he had already been home and was gone. We have an APB out extending all over the state, not just Yavapai County. He won't get away. You have my word on that!"

Patrick intervened, "Nick, what do you need from us?" He placed his hand on Laura's arm.

"I need a list of relatives or friends who might shelter Randy. I thought it would be faster coming from you, Laura. You know we're on the same side. We have enough DNA evidence to charge him. Will you help us?"

"Of course. Do you have Vicky's phone? I can go through it and give you a list right now."

When Nick left to retrieve her sister's phone, Patrick tried to console Laura. "Nick is a dedicated detective. He'll get him, I'm sure."

"This is all so surreal. My sister is dead and the man responsible is missing. I feel so helpless."

"I understand that but please, Laura, let's give Nick an opportunity to do his job. We don't want Randy to get away on a technicality because we interfered."

About that time, Nick returned and handed the cell phone to Laura. "Here it is." He also handed her a tablet and pen.

She went to work right away, ignoring the two men in the room. Nick motioned for Patrick to join him in the hallway. "Is she going to be alright?"

"This has hit her hard, as you can imagine, but Laura is a very resilient lady and eventually she'll survive this tragedy."

"You're quite taken with her, aren't you?" Nick asked.

Patrick avoided confirming the suggestion and was saved an answer when Laura joined them. "Here, it's done. Now, what else can we do?"

"You're not going to like this answer, but I just need you to let us do our job." Nick saw the look of frustration on her face.

"Come on, let's go." Patrick said.

"You keep us in the loop!" Laura looked Nick directly in the eyes.

"I wouldn't dare keep information from you. Lady, I'm not sure what you're capable of and I never poke the bear."

Once at the truck, Patrick suggested, "Want some breakfast? I have a project you could help me with afterwards, if you're interested."

"Patrick, I appreciate what you're trying to do right now, but I'm quite capable of keeping myself out of trouble. I'm sure you have better things to do than babysit me. I'm not very hungry either but I could use a cup of coffee." Laura agreed.

"I've got that at my home. Ready?"

The drive to his house was spent in silence. As he opened the door, she noticed the garage was full of wood and some unfinished cabinets. "What is all this?"

"This is the project you can help me with. I'm making these cabinets for a customer who has a mountain cabin and wants rustic cupboards in the kitchen. I know how you like to keep yourself busy when you're stressed. I thought we could work out our frustrations together."

Laura got closer, giving Patrick a big hug. "That's so thoughtful of you. You're right, I think we both need a release for our stress. Thanks."

"I can think of another way to get rid of our tensions, but I don't think our relationship is ready yet." The teasing grin on his face made her laugh out loud.

"You're right. This is a better way for now. What do you want me to do?"

"I'll finish building the cabinets, you can make the doors. I made this door to use for your pattern. All the doors are the same size."

"Oh, wow. Do I get to use power tools?" She ran her hand over the rough sawn wood.

"Absolutely. I'll be right back." Patrick disappeared through the door but was back in no time at all. He carried a tray laden with coffee cups and some pastries. "I never make a person work on an empty stomach."

"You are an amazing man." She poured coffee from the thermos for both of them. Patrick pulled up two stools and they sat next to a workbench and enjoyed their breakfast. As soon as she was done, Laura asked, "This is tongue and groove wood, isn't it? What a unique way to make these doors look rustic."

"It's knotty cedar. I like the look of it and my customer has his entire ceiling covered with the same boards. Here, let me show you how to put this door together and then you're on your own while I finish the cabinets."

She watched and asked a few questions, but soon Patrick was working on his part of the job and Laura was confidently assembling the doors. At one point, Patrick turned on some music and let the stereo surround them with melodies while they worked.

"How many of the doors do you need?" Laura asked.

"Eight should do it. I have one row of cabinets that will take six and a smaller section that will take only two. It's a small cabin and the owner doesn't want any upper cabinets, just these lower units."

"I'd like to see it. It sounds interesting."

"You can go with me when I deliver these, if you'd like." Patrick offered. They had been working for several hours and the time working on this project was calming to her nerves.

She was just about to answer when a car pulled into the drive and stopped behind Patrick's truck. Her heart sank when she saw it was the detective, Nick. "Oh, this can't be good."

Patrick came over to stand beside her as they both greeted Nick.

"I thought you should hear the news in person."

"It's not good, is it?" Laura asked the obvious.

"They found him." Nick hesitated.

"Just tell me, Nick. I can take it." Laura pressed the detective.

"Two hikers found his truck back in the woods down the Senator Highway. Randy committed suicide."

Thirteen

"That son of a bitch!" Laura exploded. "What in the hell happened?"

"I know you're upset." Nick tried to explain.

"You don't have any idea how I'm feeling! I've lost my sister to murder, now you tell me he's killed himself and you think I'm just distressed!" She stepped away from both men, not wanting them to see her tears.

"Nick, why don't we go in and get a cup of coffee. You can fill us in on all the details." Patrick went over to Laura and put his hand on her back. "I know this is very painful, but we need to find out what happened."

He saw her tears as Laura turned to face him. "These are tears of anger. That cruel man doesn't deserve tears."

As they sat at the kitchen table, Patrick tried to be the perfect host by supplying a cup of coffee and pastries for Nick. Tension filled the room as Laura waited for Nick to describe what happened.

Clearing his throat, he finally looked from Patrick to Laura and began, "By the time we arrived at Randy's house, he'd been there and left twice, leaving the house unlocked with the kitchen door wide open. There were personal belongings, paperwork, and clothing strewn about as though he was in a hurry to select certain items and avoid us."

Laura asked, "How do you know he'd been there twice?"

Nick raised his hand to stop her and in his abrupt way, said, "Let me finish and then I'll answer your questions, if I can."

Once Nick noticed Patrick and Laura nod in agreement, he continued, "Randy had been drinking. It appeared he was headed up to Interstate 40 when the police in Chino Valley stopped him for a DUI, you know, driving under the influence. This was the very night Vicky was found."

"He wasn't kept in jail." Laura stated plainly.

"No. Unfortunately, we hadn't broadcast any information about him yet, so he was only kept for a few hours and once he paid his bail, he was released. The rifle found on the seat beside him was confiscated but that was all."

Nick took a sip of his coffee. "We asked the neighbors on both sides of the house to alert us if he came back. Both neighbors called as they saw Randy pull into his drive in the early morning hours, but he didn't stay long enough for us to nab him. It seemed he just dashed in, grabbed another gun out of his gun rack and left as fast as he could. We didn't have any officer watching the house. We should have." Nick's tone showed the regret he was feeling about his decision.

"A couple of women were hiking a very remote and not well-used trail close to the old Palace Station on the Senator Highway outside of town, when they found his truck. The motor wasn't running but he had rigged tubing from the exhaust pipe into the cab."

"In his truck we found a receipt for the tubing and duct tape and a handwritten note. The gun was laying on the seat with a bullet in the chamber and two extra bullets in his pocket."

"What about the note he left?" Laura couldn't wait.

"He didn't admit anything. Randy said he was depressed and didn't want to live. Look, I know you want justice, but I can't give it to you. I wish I could, but Randy took the answers we need to his grave."

Laura was in shock. "What happens now?"

"With Randy's death, the cases on Donna Bell and your sister will be closed."

Patrick watched the emotions cross over Laura's face. He could see she was struggling to contain her anger and frustrations. "Laura?"

As Laura stood, she held out her hand to Nick. "I want to thank you for telling us this bad news in person. I've never been involved in an investigation, but thanks to Patrick's help, I've learned so much. Homicide is a lot worse than is shown on television, especially when it involves your own family. I can appreciate what you two have dealt with and seen in your careers."

"Laura?" Patrick asked once again.

"Please, can you take me home? I need to be alone for a while." Laura didn't wait for an answer but headed out to the garage. The two men followed her outside. Nick was on his phone as he left. Patrick turned to take her in his arms. His strength and warmth helped to soothe her frazzled nerves.

Once they arrived at her house, Laura stopped Patrick from getting out of his truck. "I can't thank you enough for helping me. I need time alone to get this latest news processed."

"I understand what you must be feeling. I, myself, now need to deal with a second death on a case that should have been solved sixteen years ago." His voice cracked with emotion.

Laura looked at him, "We didn't catch the bad guy, did we?"

Patrick picked up her hand and kissed it. "No, we did not, and I am so sorry."

As Laura opened the truck door and stepped out, she said, "Patrick, I think we did everything we could. It was beyond our control."

"Please call me if you need to." He waved as he drove away from the curb.

Laura finally let the tears fall. She walked to her front door and as she let herself in, took one last look at his truck driving away. We were a good team, she thought, even though we weren't successful.

As she shut the front door behind herself, Laura stood there stationary for a moment. What do I do now? Her thoughts were jumbled, as were her emotions. Laura wandered down the hallway to her office and looked at the stacks of information and evidence. "Whew." She let out a big sigh. That will have to wait, she thought.

Realizing it was around two in the afternoon, Laura went to her kitchen. She opened the refrigerator and selected a bottle of water. Before she could sit down, the doorbell rang, and she went to the front door.

"What did you forget?" Laura responded, expecting Patrick to be standing there, but was taken by surprise. "Lisa!"

"I'll bet you didn't expect to see me." Randy's daughter pushed her way into the house and shut the door.

Laura tried to regain her composure. "I guess you could say that. What are you doing here?"

"You could say my appearance on your doorstep is a complete shock, huh?" Lisa repeated her words. She appeared nervous as she gazed around the room. "Are you alone?"

Laura's suspicions were already raised but with Lisa's question, she knew that she was in trouble. Knowing her gun was in her purse on the kitchen counter, Laura started backing up toward the kitchen.

"Stop right where you are!" Lisa pulled a small revolver out of her pocket. "You need to help me and I'm not in the mood for any more delays."

"If you need my help, you don't need that." Laura pointed to the gun. "I thought you were back east somewhere." She stalled to give herself time to formulate a plan of escape.

"I do live out of state, but when my dad needs me, I'm here for him." Lisa stepped backwards toward the hallway, keeping her eyes on Laura as she quickly looked down its length. "Let's go!" Lisa waved her gun, indicating Laura should lead the way.

"Where are we going? What kind of help do you need?"

"My father wants me to get some money out of his safe but your friends, the cops, are all over his house. You need to convince them to let us get in the house." Lisa pointed to her car. "You drive. I do know how to use this, so don't try any tricks."

Just as she opened the door of Lisa's car, out of the corner of her eye, Laura noticed Sunny driving towards the house. Looking straight at Sunny, she rubbed her hand over her nose and prayed her granddaughter would understand her warning.

"Stop stalling!" Lisa shouted.

A quick glance at the road convinced Laura that Sunny recognized the message as she watched her granddaughter drive past Laura's house and pull into the neighbor's drive a few houses down.

"When did you go to your dad's house? You do realize I'm not associated with the police and they might not allow us to enter." Laura's mind was racing. Didn't Lisa know her dad was dead?

"I was there earlier this morning, but I didn't stop when I saw all those cops tearing the place apart. Don't drive so fast! I don't want to raise any suspicions."

Laura allowed her thoughts to wander. She could just imagine the conversation between Sunny and Patrick. Laura knew she would call him.

"Patrick, this is Sunny, and my Nana is in trouble. Please call me back right away!" She also sent an urgent text. Sunny had just made the decision to follow Laura when he called.

"What's going on?" Patrick demanded.

"I just saw Lisa, Randy's daughter, leading my Nana into her car. Nana gave me our signal."

"Settle down, Sunny. What signal are you talking about?" Patrick tried to get her to calm down. *"Are you sure it was Lisa?"*

"I'm positive it was her! Remember I watched the interview you two recorded? I'm going to follow them. Stay on the phone with me." As soon as she started her car, the phone switched to the car speaker, allowing Sunny to pay attention to the direction Lisa and Laura were driving.

"Sunny, you mentioned a signal from your grandmother. What does that mean?" Patrick's voice was starting to reveal the alarm he was feeling.

"When I was a young girl, Nana would rub her hand over her nose to let me know that I wasn't acting properly. If we were in a public situation, I would see that signal and know I would be in trouble if I didn't straighten up. We've kept it going all these years and I just know she's in trouble. Why else would she go somewhere with Lisa?"

"Stay far behind their car but stay on the phone and let me know where they are going. I'm on my way."

Lisa poked her in the ribs with the gun, bringing Laura back to reality. "Pay attention to your driving!"

"Lisa, when did you last talk to your father?" Laura asked.

"It was a few days ago, but we had a plan and he should be halfway to Canada by now. I'm going to get the money and meet him."

They had just turned up the street to Randy's house. As they got closer, Laura could see that the drive was empty. "There's no one here."

"Yeah, but those bastards have been here. Look at that!" Lisa pointed to the front of the garage. Plywood was nailed up where the garage door had been. "Why would they take the door?"

"Lisa, there's something you should know!"

"If you mean that horrible sister of yours is dead, I already know that! Why do you think my dad needed me?"

Laura felt like she had been punched in the gut. This woman's crazy, she thought, with a higher level of panic. Trying to stay calm, she said, "Lisa, you don't need me now. I'll just walk down to the shopping center and call my son." Laura started to climb out of the car, but Lisa was faster and came around just in time to grab her.

"My dad told me not to trust anyone, especially you! Now come on, we need to go in the house." Laura could feel the gun pressed to her back as Lisa pushed her ahead.

Once inside the house, Lisa went to the coat closet, always keeping her gun pointed at Laura. She pushed the coats aside and reached for a button near the back of the closet. A panel slid open, and a light came on, revealing a staircase leading to a lower level. Laura knew that if she went down there, she wouldn't make it out alive. Once more, she made an appeal, "Lisa, you don't need me. Get your money and get out of here! I'm not going down there."

"Oh, yes you are!" With a shove, she pushed Laura down the staircase.

Tumbling down the steps, Laura tried to save herself from serious harm. She came to rest at the bottom of the steps in an awkward position. Laura knew immediately that her right arm was fractured as the pain surged up to her shoulder. She moaned, "I think my arm is broken! Lisa, this has got to stop!" Laura wiped at blood coming from the top of her head.

"You're lucky that you only broke your arm! It saves me putting a bullet in you." Lisa was now at the bottom of the stairs. "Your sister wasn't that lucky." She said over her shoulder as Lisa went over to the gun safe on the far wall.

Laura struggled to get up from the floor when she noticed a movement out of the corner of her eye at the top of the stairs. Patrick put his finger up to his lips to silence Laura. She pointed in Lisa's direction, and he nodded. "You killed Vicky? Why?"

"She was going to leave my father and that would hurt him deeply. I love my dad and can't stand to see him sad because of a stupid woman." Lisa had her back to Laura as she opened the safe and started pulling out bag after bag of money and stacked them on the floor.

Laura watched as Patrick carefully climbed down the stairs, trying not to make any sounds. "Did you kill your mother, too?"

"Of course!" Her matter-of-fact answer chilled Laura to her core. "She was going to leave my father too. My mother wanted to take me with her, and I couldn't allow that to happen."

"What exactly happened?" Laura tried to keep her distracted while Patrick reached the bottom of the stairway and backed into the darkened space behind the stairs before Lisa was able to see him.

"I'm going to tell you only because you're going to die down here, and you won't be able to tell anyone." An evil look passed over her face as Lisa began her tale. "My dad and I went to pick my mother up after work. When we came around the corner, we saw her kissing a man. I'll never forget the look on my father's face when he saw her betrayal. He stopped the car and waited until that man left and mother started to get in her car."

Lisa seemed lost in her own memories but eventually continued. "She got in the car with us, but they argued the entire trip home. My mother was mad because my dad made her leave her car in the parking lot. She yelled that she didn't need him to pick her up from work. I put my hands over my ears, but I could still hear the hateful words she was saying."

"That must have been terrible for you." Laura empathized.

"Don't be nice to me! It's not going to change your fate. My mother tried to be nice to me. We were in the kitchen at home, just the two of us. Dad was out back trying to figure out what he was going to do. She begged me to leave with her and her new man. When I said I wouldn't leave my dad, she slapped me hard right across the face. I almost passed out from that blow. I picked up the cast iron skillet on the stove and I hit her as hard as I could."

Laura's heart ached for the thirteen-year-old girl that Lisa had been at the time. "Lisa, please help me up. This doesn't have to end with another murder."

"I'm going to meet my dad, and then I'll have the happiness I finally deserve."

"What about your husband? Won't he miss you?"

"I have no husband. I told that lie so you wouldn't be suspicious of me. After we buried my mother, my dad sent me back east to live with an old aunt. It was hell. I kept hoping he would let me come back home but then he met your sister. I was forgotten again."

By this time, Laura was sitting up. Her head had stopped bleeding, but she couldn't move her arm and the pain was unbearable. She wanted to keep Lisa talking and give the police time to get there. Laura assumed Patrick had called them.

"Lisa, your dad is dead." She waited for a reaction, but didn't have to wait long.

Lisa came over and kicked her hard in the side. "That's a lie! He's going to meet me in Vancouver. We're going to be together, just the two of us.

Just then, Patrick jumped out of the shadows and knocked Lisa down. He had his gun pointed right at her head. "I'll be the last thing you see if make a move!"

Lisa started to cry. "You didn't have to do that! I wasn't going to kill her. I just wanted to scare her."

Laura heard footsteps and suddenly the room was full of police. Nick was coming down the steps with Sunny close behind. Nick turned to her, "I thought I told you to stay up there! You're as stubborn as your grandmother."

"Nana!" Sunny was down on her knees. Tears were streaming down her young face as she tried to hug Laura. "Oh, my God, what did she do to you?"

Patrick helped Nick handcuff Lisa and hand her over to two uniformed officers to take her upstairs. "They're bringing a stretcher for you, Laura."

"I can walk if you help me up." Laura protested.

"Nana, don't even try. Let them take care of you." Sunny insisted.

"I'm so glad you got my message."

"Nana, our secret signal worked great! Are you really going to be alright?"

"Sunny, you need to let the medics take care of her." Patrick gently touched her shoulder.

"Of course, I'll be right here, Nana." She reassured Laura.

"Patrick, what will happen with Lisa?" The young girl asked.

"I'm not sure. She's a deeply troubled woman." Patrick looked around the room, watching the team of investigators gathering evidence.

"You mean she might not go to jail?" Sunny shook her head in frustration.

"Evidence is gathered and then it's up to a prosecutor to decide if Lisa can be tried for two murders. It's not like in the movies. The law can be very complicated."

"What do you mean, two murders?"

"Lisa killed her own mother. I listened as she told her gruesome story to your Nana. Let's get out of here. They're ready to take Laura to the hospital and I know you want to be there."

Taking one last look around the room, detectives, photographers, and forensic technicians were busy with activity. Patrick noticed a desk and computer in one corner. "Doesn't that just take the cake?"

"What?" Sunny asked.

"I think Lisa was living down here. See that desk over there? She was at that computer when we had our interview with her." He pointed. "That would explain why we thought someone was coaching her. It was probably Randy."

"Oh, my God, you're right. I remember that picture behind her. How weird."

As they got to the ambulance, the medics were loading Laura into the back of the vehicle. "Nana!" Sunny rushed over. "Can I ride with her?" She asked.

Looking from Laura to her granddaughter, the technician recognized the emotions between the two. "Sure. You can sit over there, but stay quiet and out of the way, okay?"

Patrick walked over to the side of the gurney. He leaned over and kissed Laura tenderly. "I'll be there shortly. I'm going to see if Nick wants my help."

A tear rolled down her cheek. "Thank you for saving me. If you hadn't showed up..." Laura stopped speaking.

"It was that special granddaughter of yours who saved you." Patrick's voice caught in his throat. "Don't give these medics too much trouble. You're in no condition to fight them."

Patrick touched her cheek but reluctantly allowed them to finish loading her into the ambulance. She could see Patrick standing there as they pulled out of the drive.

"I love you, Nana." Sunny spoke lovingly to her grandmother as the ambulance rumbled down the road.

Once at the hospital, Laura was taken into an examination room, but Sunny was told to stay in the waiting area. One of the nurses told her, "Your father is out there."

"Did you call your dad?" Laura asked.

"Yes, I knew he'd want to be here for you. I'll see you in a little bit, Nana." Sunny kissed her.

Laura didn't have time to reflect on the hell she'd just been through as nurses, technicians, and doctors came and went. Questions were asked and answered. Finally, with her arm in a cast and her head bandaged, Laura was rolled down the hall to a room. She had just closed her eyes when a light knock at the door alerted her to company.

"Mom? Oh my, you've certainly looked better." Josh and Sunny came in to visit. "Sunny said you were pushed down a stairway."

"Yes, I hit my head and broke my arm. I think I remember someone saying I had a concussion, but everything should heal in time."

"Mom, this should show you to leave the detective work to the ones who have the training." Josh admonished his mother.

"Listen here, son, I'm quite capable of taking care of myself. I'll have you know if Lisa hadn't caught me by surprise, I would have had the upper hand."

"So, it was Randy's daughter all along? Wow, I would have never figured that one out."

"I'm not sure I would have either. I mean, there was something weird about the interview we had with her, but if Lisa hadn't come over to my house, she might have gotten away with both murders." Laura took a deep breath, "I think she's nuts!"

"Patrick says the same thing. Lisa might not face charges because of her mental state." Sunny added.

"Lisa won't get away with it completely, she could be in a mental hospital for the rest of her life." Josh said.

"Nana, did you know about that secret room?"

"I had no idea. I don't think Vicky even knew about it. It's clear Randy lived a double life for sure." Laura yawned.

"Mom, we're going to go home. You need your rest. How long did they say you'd be in here?"

"They didn't. I'll be fine. I am tired." She agreed.

After they said their goodbyes, Laura was left with her own thoughts. She was feeling no physical pain, thanks to the pills the doctors had given her. Her only pain was the anguish she felt with the loss of her sister. Vicky was an innocent victim of a very sick individual and there would never be enough justice for her.

Laura had no idea how long she'd been asleep when she felt his touch on her cheek. Her eyes fluttered open and she saw Patrick's handsome face. "Hey, you look beautiful." He whispered.

"Liar." She retorted with a smile.

"How are you feeling?"

"I have to admit, I've been better. Pull up a chair." She was glad he was here. "Are the investigators done at the house?"

"I'll let Nick give you an update." At Patrick's words she looked up and saw the detective at the door.

"Come on in, Nick." Laura invited.

"I'm glad to hear that you're going to be fine." Nick said.

"I'm not easily damaged." She tried to joke.

"I've only just met you, lady, but I've come to quickly realize you are one tough woman."

"Before you start, I have a question. Why was the garage door taken down?

"I won't beat around the bush because I know you want it straight. We found blood splatters on the inside of that door. By taking the garage door down and to the lab, it can be determined where Vicky was standing when she was struck down."

Tears came to Laura's eyes as she was overwhelmed with the the mental image of Vicky's horrible death. "She wasn't shot?"

"No, why do you ask that?"

"Lisa told me that she shot her. What else have you found?"

Nick related that more money was found in the gun safe, money that was from the sale of the stolen merchandise. He said that they would spend several days gathering everything they could. "We'd like to tie Lisa to the entire situation, not just the two murders. All evidence will be assessed in an effort to do that. I know you two would like to be alone. If you have any questions, just let Patrick know and I'll get you some answers. Take care." Nick made his exit.

Patrick settled in a chair next to her bed and took her hand in his. "They're definitely going to take a couple of days. There's a lot of evidence to go through. Did you know about that room down below?"

"I had no idea and before you ask, I don't think Vicky knew anything about it."

"Do you realize that when Sunny hid in that closet, she could've stumbled on it? She would have been in more danger than we originally thought."

"Do you think Lisa was living down there?" Laura asked.

"I think it's entirely possible, but I don't know how long she was there."

"Sunny said that you think Lisa is a sick woman. Does that mean she'll get away with murder?"

"I don't think so. At the very least, she'll spend the rest of her life in a mental hospital. I know that's not the justice we would want, but at least she won't be able to terrorize anyone else." Patrick's touch on her hand was comforting, even if his words were not.

"There's something else I want to discuss with you."

"Go for it." She responded.

"I had no idea you would be in any danger. Laura, I think that in the future you should leave the detective work to me."

He didn't expect her laughter and was surprised by her reaction. "I'm serious, Laura. I don't want to expose you to more risk."

"Patrick, there's no way either one of us could have anticipated this scenario. Did you in any way, suspect that Lisa was involved?"

"Not really. After you showed me the interview again, though, I felt something was off about it. I discovered where Lisa was seated during our interview with her. She had been right there in that basement room. I saw the desk and computer over in the corner."

"Oh, my God. Vicky could have been killed at any time with Lisa living down there. That is so sick. Where do we go from here?" Laura finally asked the question that was on her mind.

"Nick will process all the information from the scene along with what we gathered. He'll present it to the prosecutor, and they'll go from there." He was the consummate professional.

"Patrick, where do we go from here?" She repeated her question.

"Oh, you mean us." He stammered.

"It's okay. You know, I'm really tired. I think they gave me some good medicine. I need to rest." Laura let him off the hook.

He stood up but hesitated, "Laura, I would have been devastated if anything serious had happened to you. I feel responsible as it is."

She held up her good hand. "Don't trouble yourself, Mister. I make my own decisions and am responsible for my own behavior and its consequences. I'll be fine, Patrick. I suggest you go home and get some rest."

"I'll see you in the morning." He kissed her on the cheek and left quickly.

The room seemed so empty without Patrick's presence. Laura adjusted her bed and pressed the call button for the nurse. She waited only a few minutes but soon her nurse appeared. "Can I help you?"

"I'm sure something was ordered for sleep. I'd like that." Laura asked.

"I can bring your medication right in. Anything else?" The nurse was efficient and professional.

"No, just that. Please."

Just then the door opened, and Patrick stuck his head in, "We did get the bad guy!" With that statement, he closed the door, leaving her to digest his comment.

Laura laid her head back and repeated his words, "We did catch the bad guy!"

Epilogue

Four Months Later

Laura set the paint can down, adjusted the bags into her free arm, rang Patrick's doorbell and waited patiently. The only conversations they'd had over the last few months were about the case. Patrick hadn't come over to her house and Laura had kept busy with everything involved in settling her sister's estate. Laura was grateful for his respect for her need for privacy, and yet she was lonely.

"Hey," Patrick said as he opened the door. "Let me help you with these things." He bent down and picked up the paint can and took several of the shopping bags from her arm. "I sense a project is about to begin."

Laura still hadn't answered him when they stopped in the kitchen and put everything on the counter. She turned to face Patrick, "I've missed you."

His response wasn't spoken as Patrick took her in his arms and kissed her eagerly. She returned his passion and blended it with her own. The heat in the kitchen wasn't from something in the oven. Finally, they pulled apart and as she looked into his eyes, Laura knew this was where she wanted to be.

Patrick asked, "Are you alright now?"

"I'm getting there. Thank you for the little notes and cards that you sent. They were so helpful each week when a new card arrived. I found myself looking forward to the next pick- me-up."

"I felt you needed your time alone as did I, but I wanted to let you know that you were on my mind each and every day."

"How are you doing? I've had plenty of time to think and it occurred to me that you must be struggling with your feelings of loss."

"You are so right. I kept thinking that if only I'd solved Donna's murder sixteen years ago, your sister would still be alive." Patrick admitted.

Laura put her fingers on his lips to silence him. "We both need to put away the 'if onlys' for now. It won't do either of us any good. We can't go back and undo our actions, but we can move forward."

"How do you propose we do that?" Patrick asked.

Laura pointed to the items on the counter. "This is the start, our new project. Let's go and clear off the wall that has Donna Bell's case on it. I've got primer paint to make a clean slate."

"And then?" Patrick prompted her to continue.

"Let's go to the office." Laura took several bags with her and Patrick grabbed the paint can and the rest of the sacks and together they went down the hallway. As he opened the door, she hesitated as a wave of emotion came over her. "I believe we need to clean this case off your walls. It will feel almost like an exorcism to get rid of that information. What do you think?"

Patrick looked at the information listed on the whiteboards and bulletin boards, then back to Laura. "I think you might be right. It'll feel great getting rid of one of these cases. Are you sure your arm is strong enough to paint?"

"Yes, it healed just fine. Fortunately, it was a clean break and with a few weeks of therapy, I'm as good as new. Let's do this!"

Together they worked removing the pictures, various papers and notes. "What do you want to do with all these things?" Laura asked.

"I have a file folder that we can put them in for now. Maybe this winter we can use all of this paper as a starter for a nice fire in the fireplace." He reached over and pulled Laura in for a comforting hug.

"Ready to take down the boards? We can get a good coat of paint on that wall for starters." Laura asked, closely watching his reaction.

"Yes, I can store these boards in the garage until I get rid of them." Patrick left the room to get his cordless drill. Once he got to work, the boards were quickly removed. "I'll give you one last chance to back out of this project. Are you sure you want to do this?"

"Of course. It won't take us long at all." Laura responded.

Like a comfortable team, they worked side by side and soon one wall in Patrick's office was newly painted and clear of any documents and evidence. Once finished, they stood back to admire their work.

"I know it's just a primer coat, but that tan color looks good, don't you think?" She asked.

"Yes, and so do you. I'm so glad you came over."

"Me, too." Laura turned and looked around at the remaining three walls of evidence. "Where do we go now?"

With a look of surprise on his face, he followed her gaze. "Are you serious? You want to do more investigating?"

"Yes, if you'll have me. I enjoy working with you and I want to try and help another family gain closure. Which case do we tackle?" Laura questioned him.

Patrick turned around and pointed. "Let's do that one. I've had some recent information on the suspect's whereabouts."

Laura moved closer to the whiteboards on that wall and studied the articles posted. "I think I remember hearing about this case. It happened in Scottsdale, didn't it?"

"Yes. Richard Foster murdered his wife and two children. He rigged the house to blow up to cover his escape. He was on the FBI's most wanted list for over twenty years, but because there's not been any new information, he's been relegated to a lower status. He's never been caught for that heinous act."

"Why is he on your list of unsolved cases?" Laura asked curiously.

"There was an unsubstantiated sighting of him in this area just a few weeks ago. I conducted some interviews, but I couldn't find anything significant at that time."

"Okay, then Richard Foster is the one. We'll get started right after this next Saturday." Laura leaned into him. "We're having Vicky's celebration of life at my house. So many friends, neighbors, and coworkers have contacted me to express their sorrow. It's comforting to see how much she was loved. Sunny, Josh and I decided we need to share that love. I hope you'll join us."

"I wouldn't miss it for the world. How about I take you out for a great dinner?" Patrick proposed.

"How about I fix us something here?" She countered.

"Let's go and search the kitchen for something to eat." They settled on a simple meal of breakfast at night. Patrick and Laura worked together and soon were enjoying their eggs and bacon.

As they cleaned up the dishes, Patrick looked out the window over the sink to see an evening storm starting up. "You don't want to get caught up in that."

Laura gave him a smile of temptation before speaking, "I thought I would stay here."

The End

About the Author

A professor on the path to her Master's degree posed this question – "If you were arrested today for something you are passionate about, would there be enough evidence to convict you?" B. B. Montgomery's passion for writing spans back to her childhood. As a human resources trainer for over 25 years as well as an instructor at the local community college, she has written numerous facilitator's guides, participant guides, and collateral pertinent to the subject being taught in her classes. She finally found the time to pursue her passion, dust the manuscripts sitting on her bookshelves, and finish what she started years ago. Yes, there is enough evidence!

For more information about BB Montgomery go to: https://www.bbmontgomery.com

Also by B.B. Montgomery

Day Trip Destiny
A Fast Affair

Ante Up Series by B.B. Montgomery
Book #1: *Love is a Dam Mystery*
Book #2: *Chasing Chips, Finding Love*
Book #3: *Spirits and Love: Rebuilding the Desperation Depot*
Book #4: *Magdalena*

Salt of the Earth Series by B.B. Montgomery
Book #1: *They Call Me Raven*
Book #2: *Saving Me and the Salton Sea*

Made in the USA
Monee, IL
22 February 2025